"*Danki*. I don't [...] **would have done** [...]

"Neighbors help neighbors," Leanna replied primly.

He understood no thanks were expected, but he also didn't like the idea of being indebted to the Waglers when he'd brought so much pain to Leanna and, through her, to her whole family.

There were many things he wanted to say to her, but he had to content himself with, "I wanted you to know Michael and I really appreciate your help."

"I'll pass your thanks on to Annie and *Grossmammi* Inez."

"Danki," he said again, though he wanted to ask why she wasn't accepting some of his gratitude for herself.

The answer blared into his head when the door closed behind her, leaving him alone with the twins. To acknowledge his appreciation would risk re-creating an emotional connection between them, one he'd thought would last a lifetime. She wasn't ready to take that chance again, and he shouldn't be, either.

So why had images of them walking together or riding in his courting buggy never stopped filling his mind during the day and his dreams every night?

Jo Ann Brown has always loved stories with happily-ever-after endings. A former military officer, she is thrilled to have the chance to write stories about people falling in love. She is also a photographer and travels with her husband of more than thirty years to places where she can snap pictures. They have three children and live in Florida. Drop her a note at joannbrownbooks.com.

Books by Jo Ann Brown

Love Inspired

Amish Spinster Club

The Amish Suitor
The Amish Christmas Cowboy
The Amish Bachelor's Baby
The Amish Widower's Twins

Amish Hearts

Amish Homecoming
An Amish Match
His Amish Sweetheart
An Amish Reunion
A Ready-Made Amish Family
An Amish Proposal
An Amish Arrangement

Visit the Author Profile page at Harlequin.com for more titles.

The Amish Widower's Twins

Jo Ann Brown

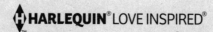
HARLEQUIN® LOVE INSPIRED®

Recycling programs
for this product may
not exist in your area.

LOVE INSPIRED BOOKS

ISBN-13: 978-1-335-47925-9

The Amish Widower's Twins

Copyright © 2019 by Jo Ann Ferguson

www.Harlequin.com

Printed in U.S.A.

Remembering mine affliction and my misery, the
wormwood and the gall.
My soul hath them still in remembrance,
and is humbled in me.
This I recall to my mind, therefore have I hope.
It is of the Lord's mercies that we are
not consumed, because his compassions fail not.
They are new every morning: great is
Thy faithfulness.
—*Lamentations* 3:19–23

For Angela Mathews.

Thanks for being such a blessing in our lives.

Chapter One

Harmony Creek Hollow, New York

"Do you sell the *milch* from your goats?"

Leanna Wagler raised her left hand to acknowledge the man's question as she continued milking Faith. The brown-and-white doe was the herd's leader and most days waited patiently while Leanna squirted *milch* into the small bucket on the raised platform. Today, the goat had taken it into her head that she didn't want to stand still.

"Just a minute," Leanna said without looking back. "I'm almost done."

It took less time than that. Drawing the pail out from under the goat, she patted Faith on the haunches, the signal the goat should jump down. Leanna set the pail on the ground and smiled as Charity, the goat who always wanted to be milked after the herd's leader, stepped up onto the platform.

"Sorry," Leanna began as she turned in the direction of the man's voice.

She didn't finish.

Instead, she stared at the man standing on the other side of the fence.

How could it be Gabriel Miller, the man who'd held her heart in his hands when she lived in Lancaster County? He'd tossed it aside to marry another woman without letting Leanna know of his plans.

It had to be Gabriel. Who else had unruly red curls that refused to lie flat in a plain haircut? His ruddy beard, still patchy, followed the strong line of his jaw. Dark brown eyes, which she had once believed were as sweet and loyal as a puppy's, widened as his gaze swept from the top of her *kapp* to the rubber boots she wore while milking.

She fought her fingers, which wanted to wipe goat hair and stains off her apron. She didn't need to try to look her best for a man who'd dumped her.

A part of her didn't want to believe the man who'd invaded her dreams, turning them to nightmares, stood in front of her. Before she could stop herself, she asked, "Gabriel?"

At the same moment, he asked, "Leanna?"

Her heart somehow managed to leap and sink at the same time. The sound of her name in his deep, rumbling voice confirmed what she'd been trying to deny.

The red-haired man in front of her was Gabriel Miller, and the *boppli* he held…

Shock pierced her again as she looked from him to the little one who had his bright red hair. Gabriel had a *kind*? She shouldn't be surprised. He'd been married for about a year and a half. The baby looked to be about six months old and regarded her with curious eyes as brown as Gabriel's.

As brown as the *boppli*'s *daed*.

Her heart broke as it had the day she'd learned he was going to marry Freda Girod.

"*Gute mariye*, Gabriel," Leanna said.

Her cool voice seemed to startle him. What had he expected? Had he thought she'd throw her arms around him or dissolve into tears? That she was tempted to do both was something he must never know.

As emotions rushed through his eyes, she waited for him to reply. He must know, as she did, that what he said next would set the tone of their future interactions. Interactions? What an unfeeling word! Yet such words would keep distance between them.

"I didn't know your Waglers lived on this farm," Gabriel said.

"We've been here over a year." She raised her chin as if she could cut the differences in their heights, for he was almost a foot taller than she was. "Are you visiting someone here?"

Please say ja, she begged silently.

"No, we've decided to become part of this new church district."

It took every bit of strength Leanna possessed to keep her shoulders from sagging at the thought of having Gabriel, his wife and their *boppli* as her neighbors. She hadn't been successful in banishing him from her thoughts. Now—seeing him at least every two weeks for church—he'd be a constant reminder of the worst betrayal she'd ever endured.

God is our refuge and strength, a very present help in trouble. That psalm, which had offered her comfort, whispered in her mind.

"Did you say something about goats' *milch*?" She remembered what he'd said, but she didn't want to talk about why he and his family had come to Harmony Creek Hollow.

He looked relieved, but didn't give her the smile that used to make her heart yearn to twirl about with joy.

He remained somber as he answered, "The *doktor* suggested goats' *milch* for my *bopplin*."

She heard a bleat from the milking platform. Charity had gotten tired of waiting and thought Leanna should know it, but Leanna couldn't move.

Couldn't speak.

Couldn't think of anything but what Gabriel had just said. He had more than the one *boppli* he held with the ease of an experienced parent in the crook of one arm?

She shouldn't be surprised. Like her, he was a twin, but unlike her and her sister Annie, he and his brother weren't identical twins. Twins were more prevalent in some families, so him being the *daed* of twins wasn't unexpected. It was a reminder, however, of how far his life had changed since the last time they'd spoken…and how little hers had.

She'd moved with her *grossmammi* and siblings, as well as her older brother Lyndon's family, from Pennsylvania to northern New York. She'd bought and now tended a herd of goats that made her laugh with their antics when she wasn't frustrated with their attempts to sneak through the fence. She had jobs cleaning houses for *Englisch* neighbors to help provide for the household.

She remained unmarried, the sole member of the friendship group she, her sister and two friends had laughingly named Harmony Creek Spinsters Club to not find a husband after moving to the new settlement. The only romance in her life, other than a few attempts by her sister at matchmaking, were the novels she read before she went to sleep each night.

She told herself to stop feeling sorry for herself. She had a *gut* life with a loving family and kind friends. She

was a member of a devoted *Leit* who came together to
worship and praise God.

"...would be better for their digestion."

Realizing Gabriel had continued talking, Leanna
struggled to listen past the roar of the windswept ocean
that had taken up residence in her head. He was going
to be living in Harmony Creek Hollow, so she must get
used to him being nearby.

But how?

Gabriel Miller wondered why nobody had warned
him Leanna was part of the Wagler family living down
the road from the farm he'd bought with his brother. Because the surname was common in Lancaster County,
he hadn't given a second thought to his new neighbors.

He should have. And maybe a third and a fourth
thought. He had no idea how he was going to get used
to having pretty Leanna right next door. When they'd
lived in Lancaster County, it had been an hour drive
from his house to hers. The last time they'd spoken, he'd
asked her to meet him at an ice cream shop in Strasburg, which was about halfway between their homes.
That had never happened. Instead, he'd married Freda.

Every time he walked out his door now, there would
be a chance he'd see the sheen of Leanna's black hair in
the sunlight or hear her soft voice lilting with laughter
and kindness. Two years ago, that would have been a
cause for celebration. Now nothing was.

A cry came from the *boppli* in his arms, and he gave
Harley a teething biscuit. The little boy chomped on it,
appeased. It was a sharp reminder, though, how Gabriel had to forget about the past and think about Harley's and his twin sister Heidi's suffering. The little girl
managed better than her smaller brother, but last night

both had been awake all night with stomachaches and vomiting. What they did get into their stomachs went through them so fast Gabriel was having a hard time keeping up with the laundry.

Thank You, Lord, he'd prayed as he had washed out diapers, tiny clothing and soiled bedding, *for having these troubles come to us in May. I don't know how we would have handled it in the middle of the winter.*

"Do you sell the *milch* from your goats?" he asked as he had before. The sooner he got his business completed, the sooner he could get out of Leanna's barnyard.

"Ja." The word seemed to spark a change in her because she lost her baffled expression and met his eyes.

For the length of a single heartbeat, it was as if he'd been thrown back in time to when he'd seen her blue-green eyes crinkling with a smile across a hay-strewn barn. *Forget that!* He couldn't let his mind get caught up in what had been. It was too late to change it anyhow.

Again he had to force himself to focus on the stumbling conversation. How easily they'd once chatted! Today, he had to weigh each word before he spoke it. Otherwise, he might utter something stupid, like the truth he had promised never to reveal.

"I'm looking to buy enough for both *bopplin*," he said. "Around three pints a day. Do your goats give enough so you can sell me that much?"

"Ja, but you'll have to pick it up. I don't have time to deliver *milch* to you." She hesitated, then asked, "Where's your farm?"

"Next door, but closer to the main road." He didn't miss how she flinched. "Michael and I purchased the farm and moved in a couple of days ago. I'd assumed I could find formula for the *bopplin*, but everything seems to upset their stomachs."

Her gaze focused on Harley again. "They may be bothered by you using different water here. Are they eating solid food?"

"Some, but we're relying on bottles for the most part. That's why it's important I get something they can keep down."

"Goats' *milch* is easy to digest." Her voice sounded normal. He wished his did. "It has less sugar and trace amounts of the protein that causes troubles for those with sensitivities to cows' *milch*. If you're going to use it as a formula substitute, though, you'll need to add in a few minerals and vitamins."

"You know a lot about this."

"My goats aren't pets. When I decided to start a herd, I did a lot of reading to know what I was getting into. I've got several customers who purchase *milch*, though they're adults, not *bopplin*."

"Gabriel…Miller…is…that you?"

He looked over his shoulder to see who was speaking in a halting manner. Again he was astonished. He'd met Inez Wagler, the matriarch of the Wagler family and Leanna's *grossmammi*, several times at haystack dinners and mud sales. The last time he'd seen her, two years ago, she'd been as spry as a grasshopper.

Inez Wagler, once a powerful oak, looked like an ancient tree stripped by a storm. She leaned on a cane as she crossed the yard toward them. Her gray hair was thin beneath her *kapp*, and wrinkles were gouged into her face. Yet, when she smiled, hints of her vibrant personality were visible.

"Gute mariye, Grossmammi Inez." He caught sight of Leanna's eyes narrowing before she turned to calm the goat vying for her attention. He shouldn't have used the name she always used when she spoke of her *gross-*

mammi. That suggested he was a member of the family, which he most definitely wasn't.

"It…is…you." She paused in front of him and rested both hands on top of the wood cane. "Are you…our new…neighbors?"

Gabriel wondered why Inez spoke in gasps. He flicked a quick glance toward Leanna and caught her unaware. Dismay was displayed across her face. As he watched, she rearranged her face into the same crisp, false smile she'd offered him.

"Grossmammi," Leanna said, "if you needed something, you could have gotten my attention from the porch."

"A soul…likes fresh…air…once in…a while." She smiled at Gabriel. "Ain't so?"

He raised his left hand as he kept Harley secure in his right arm. "I may be a new member of this settlement, but I learned long ago never to get in the middle of a disagreement between two strong-willed women."

Inez laughed and, to his amazement, Leanna did, too. He hadn't meant it as a joke.

"Who…is this…with you?" the old woman asked.

"My son, Harley." He offered her a smile, but suspected it looked as fake as it felt. "His twin, Heidi, is at home. It's a boys' trip out to buy some *milch* from Leanna's goats."

His son seemed fascinated by Inez, who spoke to him in a gentle, soothing voice. Chewing on his teething biscuit, he stared at her.

"He's…never seen…anyone…as old…as me." Inez's chuckle turned into a gasp as she struggled for breath.

Gabriel reached out to her, but she waved him away, telling him she was fine.

He didn't believe it, not when he saw the concern on

her *kins-kind*'s face. Leanna's hands were clenched into impotent fists at her sides as if she were battling with herself not to climb out of the goats' pen and come to her *grossmammi*'s aid.

"Welcome…to…Harmony…Creek. We hope… you'll…like it…here." She looked at her granddaughter. "Ain't so?"

Color rushed up Leanna's face, and he realized how pale she'd been since she discovered him on the other side of the fence. When Leanna nodded and remained silent, her *grossmammi* headed to the house. Inez halted partway and asked Leanna to come in when she was done with him.

Gabriel halted himself from saying Leanna had been done with him a long time ago. Why bring up the past when she'd made it clear with her curt comments that she hadn't forgiven him for marrying someone else?

Why should she? She hadn't replied to the letter he'd sent her before he took his marriage vows, so he'd known she hadn't been ready to grant him the forgiveness he'd asked for. She must believe he was heartless. He couldn't change her opinion, because he couldn't share the truth with anyone.

Once her *grossmammi* was out of earshot, Gabriel asked, "Why does she sound the way she does?"

"We're not sure." Leanna pushed aside the goat poking her with its head. "Her *doktor* thinks it may have something to do with one of her heart valves, so he's sending her to a cardiologist."

"I never imagined her so weak she'd need a cane."

"Me, neither." Leanna became all business, and he knew she didn't want to say more about her *grossmammi*. She told him what she charged for a quart of *milch* and what containers he would need.

"I leave for work by ten most mornings," she said, "so please be here before then. Until school is out, *Grossmammi* Inez is here by herself, and it'd be better if she wasn't disturbed."

Though questions about where Leanna worked demanded answers, he didn't ask them. "I'll make it a priority to be here before you head out. If I can't be, we'll work out something else. I appreciate you helping me, so I want to make this as easy as possible for you."

"Danki." She glanced at the black goat on the milking platform, and he knew she and the doe wanted him gone.

Had she guessed he hadn't been speaking just about picking up the *milch*? When he'd made the decisions he had almost two years ago, he'd hoped there would be a way to avoid hurting Leanna. He'd spent hours working on that letter to her, praying God would give him the right words. God hadn't listened to that prayer, as He hadn't so many others in the past year. Somehow, in the midst of his chaotic life, he'd lost his connection with God, and he wasn't sure how to find it again.

"No, I should be the one saying *'danki.'* If you didn't have *milch* to sell, I don't know where I could have found some." He backed away a couple of steps.

"There are several people around here who sell it. If you want, I can give you their names and addresses. That way if you want to check prices or—"

"I'm sure you're giving me a fair price, Leanna, and I won't find any place more convenient than next door."

"True."

When she didn't add anything else, he began to walk toward his gray-topped buggy. It'd been delivered that morning, and he had other errands before he headed home and continued unpacking enough so they could get through another day.

"Gabriel?" Leanna called.

Facing her, he asked, *"Ja?"*

"If it's easier, your wife is welcome to *komm* and pick up the *milch* for your *bopplin.*"

It was his turn to flinch.

She must have seen because she hurried to say, "Gabriel, it's okay. Tell her she and the *kinder* are welcome here anytime."

"I can't." He kept emotion from his face and his voice as he added, "I can't, because she's dead."

Chapter Two

Leanna stood by the fence and watched Gabriel's buggy drive out of sight along the curving road. She wasn't sure how long she would have remained there, frozen in the warm sunshine, if Charity hadn't voiced her impatience again.

Milking the rest of the goats took Leanna less than an hour, and she carried the *milch* into the house in two large pails. As she'd expected, her *grossmammi* was sitting at the comfortable kitchen table.

Grossmammi Inez looked up from her mending as Leanna walked past her to pour the *milch* into storage containers. Most of it went into the refrigerator to wait for customers to pick it up, but she kept some to freeze in plastic containers for when she made soap on Saturdays. She did that every other week, when a church Sunday didn't follow, because she doubted anyone would want to sit for three hours beside her when she reeked of the fragrances she used in her soap mixtures.

"Are you still going to have enough *milch* to make soap?" her *grossmammi* said, halting to take a breath after every word.

"I may have to go to a schedule of making soap

once a month." She sealed the plastic containers and marked the date on them with a wide-tipped felt pen before putting them in the freezer. "I've been making soap since I started milking the goats this spring. I should have enough to set up a table at the farmers market for June and July." She calculated in her head. "It'll work out fine, though Gabriel wants to buy three pints every day."

"With two *bopplin*, he'll need that. *Bopplin* depend on *milch* when they're young."

"He said something about them eating some solid food."

"How old are they?"

"I'd say from looking at Harley that they're around six months, but I don't know." She put the buckets in the sink and began to rinse them so they'd be ready for milking the next day. Some people milked their goats twice a day, but she'd opted for once. That allowed her time to work and help her sisters take care of the house.

"Twins usually look younger than other *bopplin*. You and your sister needed some time to catch up." *Grossmammi* Inez gave a half laugh that turned into a cough. "Not that you ever grew very tall."

"Gabriel didn't get married that long ago."

"*Bopplin* come when they want, and twins are often raring to be born. You and Annie weren't eight months in the womb before you decided you had to come out. Your *mamm* always said Annie dragged you with her because you've always had so much more patience than she does."

Leaving the buckets by the sink to dry, Leanna looked across the kitchen to where *Grossmammi* Inez's needle dipped in and out, mending a tear across the upper leg of a pair of her younger brother Kenny's barn pants. Most of her brother's work clothes were criss-crossed with repairs.

"Grossmammi?"

As she raised her eyes, her smile faded away. "Something is wrong, ain't so? You look bothered, Leanna. Is it because Gabriel and his family have moved in next door?"

"Partly." She couldn't imagine being anything but honest with her *grossmammi*.

During Leanna's childhood, *Grossmammi* Inez had taken them in twice. The first time had been following Leanna's *daed*'s death, and then the *kinder* moved in again during the horrible days after her *mamm* and beloved stepfather were killed in a bus accident on their way to a wedding in Indiana. Not once had her *grossmammi* complained about having to raise a second family in the cramped *dawdi haus* attached to her son's home.

"Then *was iss letz*?" asked the elderly woman.

"Grossmammi..." She wanted to say what was wrong was that two tiny *bopplin* would never know their *mamm*, but the words stuck in her throat. She'd never met Freda, whose family lived in another church district. Even so, sorrow surged through her at the thought of the *bopplin* growing up without their *mamm*. Crossing the room, she sat beside her *grossmammi*. She folded her hands on the table and drew in a steadying breath. As soon as she spoke the sad words, it would make them more real.

"Say what you must," *Grossmammi* Inez urged. "Things are seldom made better by waiting."

Leanna stumbled as she shared what Gabriel had told her before driving away. Tears burned her eyes, and she blinked them away. "He didn't say when Freda died, but it couldn't have been very long ago."

Her *grossmammi* regarded her steadily before saying, "You know your feelings had nothing to do with God's decision to bring Freda Miller to Him, ain't so?"

"I know." She stared at her clasped hands, not wanting to reveal how hearing Freda connected to Gabriel's surname always sent a pulse of pain through her. She'd imagined herself as Leanna Miller so many times.

Why did the thought of Gabriel married to someone else remain painful? Leanna frowned. She shouldn't be thinking of herself, only the *bopplin*. The poor woman was dead and her *kinder* were growing up without her.

"Are you upset because you think Gabriel Miller has come to Harmony Creek Hollow specifically to look for a wife to take care of his *bopplin*?"

Leanna's head snapped up at the sound of her sister's voice coming from the back door. Trust Annie, her identical twin, to get right to the heart of the matter. Her twin never hesitated to say what was on her mind.

Deciding to be—for once—equally blunt, Leanna asked, "How long have you been eavesdropping?"

"Long enough to find out who moved into the empty house next door." Annie stooped to give *Grossmammi* Inez a hug. "I came in to pick up a different pair of shoes." She pointed to her paint-stained ones. "I put the wrong ones on when I left for the bakery this morning. Before I go, though, you haven't answered my question, Leanna. Are you worried Gabriel Miller is here solely to find a wife to take care of his *bopplin*?"

Being false with her twin would be like lying to herself.

"Ja."

She watched as Annie and their *grossmammi* exchanged a glance, but couldn't read what message they shared.

Getting up, she hugged them. She retrieved her *milch* buckets from the sink and took them out to the shed before hitching the horse to their buggy. Today was her day to clean Mrs. Duchamps's house, and she needed to hurry or she'd be late.

The questions her family had asked were a wake-up call. She must not let the lingering longings of her heart betray her more than Gabriel had.

What was he doing wrong?

Gabriel looked from the handwritten recipe on the battered wooden counter to the ingredients he'd gathered to make formula for the twins. Realizing he'd missed a step, he added two tablespoons of unflavored gelatin. As he stirred the pot, he frowned. Something wasn't right. The color was off, and it was getting too thick too fast. He tried a sip. It tasted as it was supposed to, which was without a lot of flavor. He guessed, once they sampled this mixture, the twins would be more eager to eat solid foods.

A quick glance across the crowded kitchen reassured him the *bopplin* were playing on the blanket he'd found at the bottom of a box marked "kitchen" and "pots and pans." Friends had helped them pack, and he guessed one person had filled the box and taped it closed before another person labeled it. Bath supplies had been discovered in a box marked "pillows." True, there had been one small pillow in it, but the majority of the box had been stuffed with shampoo, toothpaste and the myriad items the *bopplin* required, including extra diaper pins.

The house, which would need his and his twin's skills to renovate, was stuffed with boxes. He and Michael had brought the barest essentials with them, including their tools. However, two *bopplin* didn't travel without box after box of supplies and toys and clothing.

He should be grateful the boxes covered up the deep scratches in the uneven wood floors. Other boxes were set to keep the *kinder* from reaching chipped walls and floor molding. An old house could be filled with lead paint.

Eventually, it would become a *wunderbaar* family home, because the rooms were spacious. Large windows welcomed the sunlight. There were three bathrooms, one on the first floor and two more upstairs amid the six bedrooms. One toilet upstairs had plumbing problems, but the water had been turned off before damaging the floors or ceilings. Some furniture had been left behind by the previous owners, but, other than the kitchen table and chairs, it needed to be carted to the landfill because it reeked of mold and rot.

Gabriel paused stirring the formula as Heidi began to clap two blocks together and gave him a grin. Her new tooth glittered like a tiny pearl. Beside her, Harley lay on his back, his right hand holding a teething biscuit while his other hand gripped his left toes. He rocked and giggled when his sister did. With their red hair and faint beginnings of freckles across their noses, they looked like a pair of *Englisch* dolls. Their big brown eyes displayed every emotion without any censoring.

Had he ever been that open with others?

It seemed impossible after the tragedies of the past couple of years.

"What a *schtinke*," said his brother, Michael, as he walked into the kitchen through the maze of unpacked or half-unpacked boxes. Pausing to wave to the *bopplin*, who giggled, he added, "I hope it tastes better than it smells, or the kids won't drink it."

"I sampled a bit of it, and it doesn't taste as bad as it smells."

"I don't think anything could taste that bad." He reached for the *kaffi* pot.

Gabriel motioned for his brother to pour him a cup of *kaffi*, too. He was becoming dependent on caffeine. When was the last time he'd gotten a full night's sleep? "If this doesn't work for them, I don't know what will."

"Why not be positive? Isn't that what you always say?"

He watched Michael fill the cups and add a touch of cream and sugar to each. He and his brother weren't identical twins. There never had been any trouble telling them apart, but the physical differences had grown more pronounced as they grew older.

Michael's hair wasn't flame red. Instead it was a darker brown with a faint tinge of russet that became, in the summer sunshine, more pronounced. He was several inches taller than Gabriel and had a nose someone once had described as aristocratic. Gabriel wasn't sure what that was supposed to mean, but he'd always admired his brother's strong profile, which was not softened by a beard, for his brother remained a bachelor. Like Gabriel, he had hands calloused from work. His fingers, which were broader than Gabriel's, could handle a plank of wood as delicately as if it were glass. He'd worked as a finish carpenter in Pennsylvania while Gabriel had focused on rough-in work.

There were more subtle differences, too. Gabriel was the steady one, the person anyone could go to when things were getting rough. He'd give them a well thought-out solution after deliberating on it. Michael jumped into any situation. As a boy, Gabriel had read comic books with an *Englisch* friend, and Michael had reminded him of a superhero who never hesitated to run toward trouble. Gabriel saw himself more as the person picking up the pieces after the super-villain had been defeated.

"Here you go," Michael said, holding out a cup.

"Danki." Gabriel continued stirring the goats' *milch* formula while they talked about the job they'd been hired for next week.

The small project, rebuilding a garage in the tiny town of West Rupert, Vermont, about six miles east, was a beginning. They'd need as much work as they could get because they'd arrived too late to get a crop in this year.

Gabriel stared into the pot. "I don't think it's supposed to be this thick."

"You should ask the person you're getting the *milch* from. Maybe he'll know."

"She. Leanna Wagler."

His brother's brows rose in surprise. "The same Leanna Wagler you met in Pennsylvania?"

"One and the same." He didn't add she'd wandered through his daydreams almost every day since he'd last seen her. "I knew she'd moved with her family away from Lancaster County, because her brother was eager to get out of that meat-processing plant and wanted a farm of his own."

"And she was eager to get away from you."

"Ha ha," he said without humor. He didn't want to give his brother's teasing comment any credibility although, with a sinking feeling, he wondered if it were true.

No! He wasn't going to add another layer of guilt to the burden he carried.

Michael whistled a long note. "Talk about coincidences! Who would have guessed you'd find the one who got away here?"

"She's not the one who got away."

"Okay, she's the one who let you get away when you decided to marry Freda instead." Slapping Gabriel on the shoulder, he asked, "Do you think Leanna wants you back?"

"No." The answer burst out of him.

Seeing Michael's *gut* humor become astonishment, Gabriel didn't want to hear another lecture on how he should get on with his life. Why did everyone seem to think they could tell him what to do? How many people had told him the *bopplin* needed a *mamm*? He was fumbling through each day, trying to be a competent *daed* as well as a *gut* business partner for his brother. He wasn't succeeding at either because he snatched only a few hours of sleep each night. Even on the nights when the twins slept through, his conscience kept him awake with questions about how he could have failed to notice Freda's despair before she died.

He set the pot aside to cool, then joined his brother at the table, selecting a seat where he could keep an eye on the *bopplin*. Wanting to talk about anything but Leanna, he asked, "Have you found the rest of our tools yet?"

"Most of them. I dug the nail gun out of a box marked 'curtains.'" He laughed. "That's not close!"

Michael didn't seem to notice when Gabriel remained silent. Had his brother gotten accustomed to Gabriel's inability to smile and laugh? Gabriel hadn't been able to remember the last time he'd done either; yet, seeing Leanna today resurrected memories of the times they'd shared a laugh together. It was shocking to think a part of him had died along with Freda, and he hadn't realized that until he'd looked into Leanna's *wunderbaar* eyes and recalled when his biggest concern had been if he'd have the courage to ask her to let him drive her home.

"Have you found someone to take care of the kids while we're at work?" Michael asked, yanking Gabriel out of his thoughts.

"Not yet."

"Our job begins a week from yesterday."

"I know."

"It's going to take two of us to get that foundation straight again. Or as straight as we can get it after the garage has been leaning for the past fifty years."

"I know," he repeated.

"Benjamin Kuhns—he and his brother run the sawmill—mentioned his sister used to be a nanny for an *Englisch* family. Maybe she'd be interested in the job."

"Maybe." He hated the idea of leaving Harley and Heidi with a stranger.

"How about Leanna? You know her. Do you think she'd be willing to watch the kids?"

"She said she already has a job."

"Doing what?"

"I didn't ask."

Michael arched that expressive eyebrow again. "What did you two talk about? Certainly not about old times."

"We talked about her selling me her goats' *milch*."

Harley let out a cry and Gabriel jumped to his feet, almost grateful for the interruption despite being worried about why Harley was crying. The *boppli* was far quieter than his sister, who wanted everyone to know when she was upset.

His anxiety eased when he realized the tiny boy had lost his hold on his toes and was frustrated with trying to capture them again. Kneeling, Gabriel guided Harley's foot toward his fingers. The *boppli* grabbed them and gurgled with contentment. Gabriel gave the *kinder* kisses before standing again.

"You're going to spoil them," Michael said with a fake frown. "Aren't *daeds* supposed to set rules for their *kinder*?"

He mumbled something in response. It must have satisfied his brother because Michael turned the discussion to the list of supplies they'd need before they began their first job.

Gabriel went to check on the formula. He kept his back to his brother, not wanting his expression to give any hint to the truth nobody living except him knew. He wasn't the *bopplin's daed*.

Chapter Three

Leanna shouldn't have felt so proud of herself. She was well aware of the fact *hochmut* was wrong for a plain person, but she couldn't help congratulating herself for treating Gabriel as she would have any customer.

For the past four days, Gabriel had come to the house every morning to collect *milch* for his *bopplin*.

For the past four days, she'd asked him how the *kinder* were, and if he and Michael were getting settled in their new home.

For the past four days, he'd given her trite answers and she'd accepted them before watching him leave.

All nice and as indifferent as if they'd met for the first time when he came to inquire about purchasing *milch*. Because, the truth was, she wasn't sure if he was the same man she'd known two years ago. The thought almost brought an ironic laugh from her as she finished milking the last goat in the pen.

If she'd known Gabriel as well as she'd thought she had two years ago, she wouldn't have been blindsided by him marrying someone else.

Hearing the rattle of buggy wheels, Leanna pushed her way out of the pen. She put down the buckets to double-check the gate was secured. Goats were escape artists, and she didn't want to give them any opportunity to sneak out.

Either she was late this morning or Gabriel was early. Usually she had the *milch* portioned out before he arrived.

She waited to cross the driveway until he'd slowed the black horse pulling his buggy. When he stepped out, he didn't wave to her. Instead, he turned to look inside the vehicle. Had he brought the *bopplin* with him? If so, it was the first time since he'd come to see if she'd sell him *milch*.

Setting the buckets on the back porch, she went to the buggy. Two car seats had been secured to the back bench. She could see tiny wiggling feet, but not their faces because the seats were set so the *kinder* looked toward the rear. Families carried their littlest *kinder* on the laps of parents or older siblings. She'd never given any thought to how *bopplin* would travel with only a driver.

"May I see the twins?" she asked.

"Sure."

She unlatched the door and started to raise it. When she stood on tiptoe to stretch it over her head, he took it and lifted it up to its full extent. Having him stand so close threatened to sweep her breath away, and she had to focus on breathing in and out so he wouldn't notice he still had that effect on her. She didn't want him to think she was a *dummkopf* for not ridding herself of her attraction for him. If only it were as easy to turn off as the lights on his buggy...

"Oh, my!" she gasped when she saw the *bopplin*. Both had inherited Gabriel's red hair, and they regarded her with big, brown eyes so much like his. "They're cute!"

"I think so."

"Of course *you* do. You're their *daed*."

"*Ja*, there's that."

She tore her eyes from the adorable youngsters to look at Gabriel. When he didn't smile, she wondered if she'd offended him with her praise. He'd never been stiff-necked before. He'd been an open book when she first met him.

Her smile vanished as she reminded herself that wasn't true. She'd fooled herself then about him, believing she'd known him when she hadn't. Otherwise, why had she assumed he cared about her?

How wrong she'd been!

She blinked hot tears as she focused on the kids again. Harley was dressed in a loose garment that would make changing his diapers easier. The little girl wore a white *schlupp schotzli*, a tiny pinafore apron, over a dark blue dress. The little girl grinned and made gooing sounds. Leanna was lost as the *boppli*'s smile warmed her heart, which had been as cold as winter since she'd heard about Gabriel's plans to marry.

Not waiting to ask Gabriel's permission, Leanna reached in and began to unbuckle the little girl. He started to do the same for Harley. Both kids bounced with their excitement at being released from the seats.

Leanna cradled the little girl for a moment before the active *kind* wanted to sit up. Balancing the *boppli* on her hip as she once had done her youngest sibling, she let herself enjoy the moment. Kenny was twelve now. She'd held plenty of other *kinder* since then, but there hadn't been the same knowing that having this *kind* in her arms was meant to be.

Until now.

"Her name is Heidi," Gabriel said, helping her shove

away the thought that should never have come into her mind.

"Harley and Heidi. Those aren't common names."

"My *daed*'s *grossdawdi* was named Harley, and my *mamm*'s great-*aenti*'s name was Heidi. From what I've been told, she was given that name because it was her *mamm*'s favorite story growing up."

Curious why both twins had been named for Gabriel's family instead of one for Freda's, Leanna didn't want to ruin the moment by reminding him of whom he'd lost. "Keeping a name alive in a family is a nice way to honor those who came before us. Annie and I were named for *Grossmammi* Inez's favorite *aentis*. It created a connection for us though they died before we were born."

She stiffened as she realized what she'd said.

He cupped her shoulder with his broad hand, creating another unexpected connection. "Don't think you have to choose every word so it won't remind me of Freda's death. I can't forget it."

"I'm sorry. I know it's impossible to forget such a loss."

Gently squeezing her shoulder, he said, "*Danki*. I'm sorry you, too, learned about such losses when you were young." He lifted his fingers from her shoulder, and the bridge between them vanished. "Can we get the *milch*? I know you don't want to be late for work."

Leanna motioned for Gabriel to come inside. He lowered the buggy's back and latched it, then followed her. She paused by the steps and looked at the forgotten *milch* buckets. Her mind was in such a turmoil she couldn't think of how to handle both of them while she held Heidi.

"You get one, and I'll get the other," Gabriel said from behind her.

"*Danki*."

She used the time it took to walk up the steps and through the mudroom to try to compose herself. When she entered the kitchen where her family was finishing breakfast, *Grossmammi* Inez looked past her to smile at Gabriel. Annie arched a single brow and remained silent.

Juanita, who at fourteen was already taller than her older sisters, came forward to take Heidi so Leanna could divide up the *milch*. Cooing at the little girl, Juanita and Kenny made faces to make the *bopplin* laugh.

Leanna's arms felt empty as she put her pail next to the one Gabriel had carried into the house. She poured out the *milch* and stored the amount she had left over for making soap in the freezer. She put the small containers she'd filled for Gabriel on the counter.

He reached for them, then halted. "I need some advice on making the formula. When I follow the recipe, it comes out so thick the *bopplin* have real trouble sucking it from the bottle."

"Do you have a bottle with you?"

He held up a finger, then rushed out of the kitchen. Returning before she'd finished rinsing out the buckets, he checked the room to see who was holding his *kinder*, and his shoulders relaxed when he saw they were still being entertained by Juanita and Kenny. He was a *gut daed*.

Then his eyes caught hers. So many questions raced through his gaze, questions she wasn't ready to answer. To do so would upset the fragile status quo, and doing that could make the situation more uncomfortable.

If possible.

Gabriel cut his eyes away before Leanna discerned too much about the secrets he hid. She'd always known what he was thinking and feeling before he did. Before, it had been charming. Now it could destroy the rickety sculpture of half-truths he'd built to protect those he'd promised he'd never hurt.

"Let me see the bottle," Leanna said, holding out her hand.

He gave it to her and watched as she tilted it and tried to sprinkle the formula into the sink. Nothing came out. She righted the bottle and walked into the living room. She got a needle from a sewing box beneath what looked like the beginning of a quilt top, and he recalled how she'd talked about quilting. She'd been especially fond of patterns that were challenging for a left-handed needleworker.

What else had he forgotten about her in the mad rush to become a husband and a *daed*?

Hearing Heidi squeal with delight from where she sat on Inez's lap while the woman who must be Leanna's twin held Harley, he relaxed again.

"You need a bigger hole in the nipple," Leanna said, pulling his attention to her, "so the *bopplin* don't have to work so hard to get the *milch* out." She used the needle to demonstrate, sticking it in and wiggling it about to enlarge the hole.

"That's a *gut* idea." He took the bottle and tried getting the formula out again. As before, nothing emerged. "It's still too small."

Her forehead threaded. "It should have worked. It's what others have done when their *bopplin* have had trouble with formula. Are you sure you're making it correctly?"

"I'm following the recipe I was given by the *doktor*'s office." He fished a copy out of his pocket. He'd been carrying it with him in the hope he could find someone to watch the twins before he had to go to work in

West Rupert in a few days. So far his search had been unavailing.

"Let me see it. Maybe I can figure out if there's a problem."

At Leanna's words, laughter burst from everyone in the kitchen.

When Inez's laugh was cut short by her uneven breathing, Gabriel found a glass and filled it with water. He set it in front of her, far enough away that Heidi couldn't grab it.

"Danki," she said in a raspy whisper. She flashed a loving smile toward her *kins-kind.* "You don't want to ask Leanna to help mix up the formula."

"Why not?"

"What my *grossmammi* is saying," Leanna interjected with a wry glance at Inez, "is that I don't cook."

He was shocked. He'd never met a plain woman who made such a claim. Most Amish families considered the kitchen the center of family life, and the women wanted to fill it—and those who entered it—with delicious food.

"Not at all?" he asked.

"Not much. Despite what the rest of the family thinks, I can cook a few things. My sisters have always enjoyed cooking, so while they've made our meals I've handled other chores around the house. However..." She flashed a jesting frown at her sisters and brother. "I can read a recipe."

More laughter swirled around the kitchen before her younger sister and brother left to get ready for school. Footsteps pounded up the stairs at the same time the first-floor bathroom's door closed.

Despite their teasing, when Leanna took the recipe and began to prepare the formula, she seemed far more competent than he was. He wondered if he was supposed to help her or if he should offer to take over for Inez and Annie, who were feeding the twins small bites of oatmeal from a bowl set between them. He halted himself before he warned them about the *bopplin* eating cows' *milch*. They knew that.

Leanna put water in a pot and reached for the box of gelatin. She spooned out two small spoonfuls.

"No," he said. "That's not enough."

"What?" She pointed to the recipe. "It's the right amount. This says two teaspoons."

He stared at the piece of paper. "Teaspoons? I thought it said tablespoons."

"No wonder the formula is so thick. You put in three times too much gelatin."

"That would do it, ain't so?" Shaking his head, he wondered what other mistakes he'd made when he was too tired to think straight.

Inez pushed herself to her feet. Keeping her hands on the table to hold herself steady, she said, "You're a busy man, Gabriel." He wanted to hug her for comprehending what he couldn't bring himself to say. "If you want, I can make up the formula and send it with Leanna each day."

He looked at Leanna. For a moment, he thought she was going to protest, but she was silent, not wanting to gainsay her *grossmammi*. Leanna always had been careful of what she said, thinking before she spoke. Another thing that hadn't changed, which pleased him. He'd respected her for not reacting to everything said or done around her, as others did.

But someone had to this time.

"That's not necessary, Inez," he said. "I can stop by and get it."

"Nonsense! She drives right past your house on her way to work."

"Where do you work?"

"I do housecleaning for several *Englisch* families in Salem," Leanna replied. "I'll be able to drop off the formula every day, except Sunday, as long as I can have access to your refrigerator."

"I'll make sure whoever I get to watch the *bopplin* knows you're coming by."

"Watching the *bopplin*?"

"You didn't think Michael and I are taking them to work with us, did you?"

When Leanna looked at him with hurt in her eyes, he knew he should have been more like her and thought before he blurted out. Rather than question her, he should have been grateful that she'd agreed when her *grossmammi* had volunteered her. Not having to go to the Waglers' farm every morning would allow him to spend a few extra minutes with the twins.

"Who's doing that?" *Grossmammi* Inez asked.

"I'm not sure," he had to admit. "Do you know someone who would be *gut* with them? I'd heard about a couple of people, but they can't help now."

"Let me think and ask around."

"Danki." He prayed Inez would find someone, because he wasn't sure what he was going to do when Monday rolled around and he had to be at work in West Rupert.

The door was barely closed behind Gabriel and Kenny, who'd offered to carry one of the *bopplin* out to the buggy, when *Grossmammi* Inez sighed and said, "That poor man needs help. Someone must step up."

"I will," Juanita said as she reached for her bonnet so

she and Kenny could head to school once he returned from helping Gabriel.

"You've got to graduate first." Leanna put her arm around her sister's shoulders.

"I will be soon!"

"I know. It's *gut* of you to offer, but he needs help now."

"True, but who's going to help him?" her younger sister cried out in frustration.

"I will."

Leanna clamped her hands over her mouth as everyone in the room turned to stare at her. She'd never said anything about her attraction to Gabriel to her family, because that was a topic never discussed until a wedding was announced. Still, everyone in her family had to have been aware of how she wanted to be with Gabriel. Nobody could have missed how she'd deflated when tidings of Gabriel's plans to marry Freda were announced.

"You?" Annie asked, wiping her hands on her apron. "Are you sure about this, Leanna?"

"He needs help. Those *kinder* have to have someone to watch over them. I can do that." *I may even be able to find a way to forgive him.* Pretending she didn't care about him and was interested in marrying someone else hadn't worked to end the disquiet in her soul. Maybe letting go of her anger would ease the blight burning inside her and eroding her happiness.

"What about your cleaning jobs?" Kenny asked as he walked in and picked up his plastic lunch container.

"What about your goats?" Juanita grabbed her own lunch box.

"What about *you*?" Annie grasped Leanna by the shoulders. "Are you going to get more involved with Gabriel and his family?"

"Enough!" *Grossmammi* Inez tapped her cane against the floor. "God guided Gabriel to Harmony Creek. It must have been because He knew there would be people here to assist Gabriel with his twins. We can't step aside when God gives the opportunity to be His servants in helping our neighbors."

Leanna flushed. "I didn't offer because—"

"Why you offered matters less than that you did offer, Leanna. Fixing the details can wait. Get Gabriel in here so we can talk about it with him." She waved a wrinkled hand toward the door. "Hurry! I hear his buggy leaving."

Leanna obeyed, though every cell in her body protested chasing after Gabriel's buggy. As she ran out of the house, she wondered if someone falling off a building felt like she did. She couldn't fight the idea she was rushing headlong into her doom, but how could she do nothing when those adorable *bopplin* needed someone to watch them?

She doubted she would have caught up enough for him to hear her shouts over the clatter of the wheels on the stones if their puppy, Penny, hadn't raced past her, barking.

When Gabriel slowed the buggy so he didn't hit the dog, Leanna shouted. He drew in the horse. As the buggy rolled to a stop, she ran to the driver's side.

"Is something wrong?" he asked. "Is it your *grossmammi*?"

"She's fine." She panted between each word. "She sent me to ask you to come back."

"Why?"

"Let's talk in the kitchen."

Her younger brother and sister nudged each other and grinned as they walked past the buggy. They thought she'd stepped up to help because she had a crush on Gabriel. Would they understand if she explained she saw this as a way to get him out of her heart?

Leanna hoped Gabriel hadn't noticed her siblings' silliness. He motioned for her to step out of the way so he could turn the buggy toward the house.

Minutes later, she was holding Harley in the kitchen while Annie kept Heidi entertained with a game of peekaboo. Gabriel stood by the table and looked from her *grossmammi* to her, perplexed.

When *Grossmammi* Inez motioned, Leanna said, "Gabriel, we know you need help with your *kinder*. We've come up a solution we hope will work for you. Juanita wants to help once school is out."

"When's that?"

"A little over two weeks. Until then," she said quickly before *gut* sense halted her, "I'm willing to step in. I can milk my goats before I go to your house, and I can find someone to take over my cleaning jobs."

"The rest of us will pitch in," Annie said, not pausing in her game with Heidi. "So do you want Leanna's help now and Juanita's later?"

"I do," he replied, his voice thick with relief.

Leanna blinked back abrupt tears when she heard Gabriel speak the words she had longed to hear him say, though not standing in her family's kitchen with his two *kinder*. She had to forget that absurd fantasy of having a happily-ever-after with him if she wanted to make this temporary situation work. She wasn't sure how she was going to let that dream go, but she must.

Chapter Four

Four hours of sleep…

He would have settled for three.

In a row.

Gabriel stared at the blackened pan and wondered how he could have fallen half-asleep standing by the stove. The four eggs he'd been frying looked as if they'd been dunked in soot. Smoke hung in the air, though he'd opened the kitchen window over the sink. Beneath heavy eyelids, he considered the stacks of dishes waiting to be washed. Maybe the smoke couldn't find its way past them.

Now there was another to add to the ones he needed to scour. He should have known better than to offer to make breakfast when he couldn't string two thoughts together.

Freda would have been horrified by the state of the kitchen. His late wife had jested over and over she wanted a house where a speck of dust wouldn't feel at home. After she'd died, Gabriel had wondered if she'd been joking. She had insisted on everything being in its place. A single glass askew in a cupboard had bothered her so much she couldn't eat before straightening it. The slightest disruption in her day sent her into a dark mood he couldn't draw her out of until she was ready to emerge.

When he and Michael had first gone to live with Freda's family after their own parents died, Freda Girod had been a happy little girl. Like her daughter, Heidi, she'd always found fun in every experience.

The Girod family had lived on the neighboring farm, so it had been a simple transition for the Miller twins to move next door. When the Miller farm was sold, the community had assumed the money would be used to raise the eight-year-olds. Instead, Aden Girod, Freda's *daed*, had put the funds into the bank and brought up the two boys along with his daughter, who was four years younger.

The money, which Aden had called their inheritance, was to be put toward buying a farm for the twins to share. He'd refused to let either Gabriel or Michael use it to help offset his medical bills piling up on the small table in the kitchen. The cancer treatments would be covered by the community, and Aden wanted "his boys," as he'd always called them, to have a *gut* start in life with a farm of their own.

Then, one night, Aden had asked Gabriel to take a walk with him along the line of trees separating the Girod farm from the one where the Miller twins had been born. He had something he wanted to discuss with Gabriel. Jumping at the chance to talk alone with the man he considered his *daed*, Gabriel had decided it would be the perfect time to tell Aden about his hopes of marrying Leanna Wagler.

He never had the chance.

Aden had opened the conversation by saying if Gabriel married his daughter, the Girod farm would be his when Aden died from his cancer, as his *doktors* feared would happen within the year. The inheritance money from the twins' parents could then be Michael's, and perhaps he could find a nearby farm so the brothers could raise their *kinder* together.

When Gabriel asked why Aden was making such an extraordinary offer when he had a daughter to inherit his farm, he'd answered, "Because I want my *kinskinder* to grow up on a family farm as my daughter did. There's not much time left to make sure that happens."

"The *doktors* have been wrong before," Gabriel had begun.

"I'm not talking about my cancer. I'm talking about Freda's situation." His voice had dropped to a whisper. "I know I should have been stricter with her when her *rumspringa* friends started spending time with *Englisch* boys."

Gabriel had almost asked when that had begun but didn't, ashamed to admit he'd been so caught up with his courtship of Leanna he hadn't been paying much attention to anything else. "You're a *gut daed*, Aden," was all he'd been able to find to say, eager to finish discussing Aden's daughter and move the conversation to discussing asking Leanna to marry him.

"If I'd been a better *daed*, maybe Freda wouldn't be pregnant."

"Pregnant?" That had stopped Gabriel in his tracks.

"The *Englischer* who she says is the *daed* has refused to marry her." He turned to face Gabriel. "How can I accept God's will that I soon will depart from this world when I have to leave my daughter in such a predicament on her own?"

"I'm so sorry." Then he'd spoken the words that shattered his dreams. "If there's anything I can do to help, ask."

"I'm glad you feel that way. Will you marry Freda and give her *kind* a name?"

The earth seemed to sway in every direction as Gabriel had stared at the old man's face. Seeing the last remnants of hope there, Gabriel hadn't been able to ask why Aden hadn't talked to Michael instead of him. Maybe Aden had. No, he'd corrected himself. Aden understood the Miller boys well, and he'd known Michael wasn't interested in farming.

Gabriel had found what he wanted, too: a life with Leanna.

But everyone said Aden Girod hadn't hesitated to take in two orphans when he'd buried his own wife a few years before. How could Gabriel say no to what might be a dying man's final request?

Nobody had seemed surprised when Gabriel and Freda's wedding plans were published at the next church Sunday. If there were whispers about how they were married outside of the usual wedding season in the late fall, he'd never heard them. That they remained at the Girod house instead of traveling to visit friends was accepted, too, because Aden's condition didn't improve, and he would need their help more than ever.

Leanna had vanished out of his life. The letter he'd written to her to explain why he'd done what he had— though he'd never mentioned Freda being pregnant because Aden had asked him never to tell anyone, not even his twin brother—hadn't brought any response. Had it been delivered? Should he have sent another?

He hadn't had a chance to decide because Aden had taken a turn for the worse, and Freda's morning sickness hadn't abated. He'd thought about talking to his brother about his concerns, but hadn't because Michael would urge him to pray to God for strength. Faith seemed so simple to his twin. To be honest, it had seemed simple to Gabriel, too, before his whole life started spiraling downward after the *bopplin* were born. Freda had become withdrawn, and he'd assumed it was because she was exhausted from giving birth and having to take care of the twins only weeks after her *daed* had succumbed to the cancer he'd been fighting for five years.

Gabriel had offered to get a *boppli* nurse to assist Freda, but she'd refused, saying she didn't want anyone coming into her house and changing things. His insistence the girl would do as Freda requested hadn't changed his wife's mind. When she had burst into tears the third time he made the suggestion, he gave up, fearing he was causing her more distress with his persistence.

That had been his first mistake, but he believed his second had been his assumption God was going to help Freda. Instead, she'd died, and Gabriel had been left with two tiny *bopplin* and a wagonload of guilt. One thing Aden hadn't ever spoken of, because it didn't need to be said, was his deep wish his *kins-kinder* be raised with two loving parents as neither Freda nor Gabriel and his brother had.

When Michael had suggested they move to the new settlement where they could leave the grief behind them, Gabriel had agreed. Anything to get away from the familiar sights that were tainted by sorrow.

Now…

A quiet knock came from the back door, jerking Gabriel out of the vicious circle of his memories. He looked up to see Leanna waiting on the other side. A quick glance at the clock over the stove told him she was right on time as usual. He'd wasted too much time reliving the past when he should be focused on the future for his family.

Leaving the blackened pan on the stove and picking up Heidi before she could crawl out of sight under the table, he was glad that while he was lost in his thoughts she hadn't decided to go into the front room again and try to lift herself up on the stack of unpacked boxes. If they fell on top of her, she could be hurt, but there was no way to explain the danger to a young *kind*. He saw Harley was right where Gabriel had put him before starting what was supposed to be breakfast. At least one of the twins was a content *boppli*.

He hoped no signs of his recent thoughts were visible when he opened the door. As he did, smoke whirled in a crazy dance through the kitchen. He couldn't help seeing how Leanna grimaced as the stench of burnt food struck her. He wanted to assure her the place didn't always look and smell so bad, but he didn't have the energy.

He said, "*Komm* in."

Waving away wisps of smoke trying to exit around her, Leanna entered. She set down a basket holding formula bottles before she lifted off her black bonnet. Her crisp white *kapp* popped into its heart shape, which accented her pretty face. In her neatly pressed pale pink dress and black apron, she seemed out of the place in the chaos. He thought he remembered seeing the ironing board in one of the unused bedrooms upstairs, but it was useless without an iron. Did he have any idea which box it might be in?

She looked well rested, too. Like his brother and the *bopplin*, who somehow had figured out how to make short spurts of sleep work. He had to be happy the only mirror in the house was the tiny one over the bathroom sink he and Michael used when they shaved. Michael complained about its size, but, for Gabriel, who only had to shave his upper lip and cheeks, it was fine. He wouldn't have wanted to see his sleep-deprivation next to Leanna's neat appearance this morning.

Had he'd remembered to shave this morning? He ran his fingertips over the stubble on his left cheek. No, he'd forgotten again. Unlike men with darker hair, his russet beard was uneven and resembled an unshorn sheep losing its winter fleece. And combing his hair? He'd forgotten that, too, which meant clumps stood up as if he'd tried to catch a bolt of lightning.

"Gute mariye," Leanna said with a smile for Heidi, who returned it with a giggle. "You look ready for trouble this morning."

"She is." Gabriel was relieved Leanna acted as if she hadn't been surprised to discover him looking unready for the day. He could play along, too, though he hated the idea they were pretending instead of living their lives honestly. "Harley is a *gut boppli*, happy to play where he's put. Heidi is our explorer. I've had to keep a close eye on her to make sure she stays away from unpacked boxes."

"Maybe she wants to help." Leanna smiled, but her expression froze when he didn't return it. Walking past him, she went to the refrigerator. She opened it and put the bottles of formula inside. She glanced at the stove and the pan where he'd burned breakfast.

He wanted to kick himself. Would it have hurt him to give her a smile? Maybe, because it could have opened him up to feelings he shouldn't have for her any longer. Those feelings were another secret he couldn't share. How many more secrets could he keep before he burst wide open and revealed the web of half-truths he'd created?

"Where's your brother?" Leanna asked, breaking the silence.

"He went into Salem to check on our order at the hardware store. We need to make sure it's delivered on…" His words faded into a yawn. When she looked over her shoulder, he apologized.

"There's no reason to say that," she said so quickly he had to wonder if she was talking about his yawn or their combined pasts. "You've got every reason to be tired. You've just moved in, and you have two *bopplin* to take care of. I don't think anyone will be running to the bishop with complaints about you yawning in the middle of a sentence."

"Or having a house that looks as if a tornado came through?"

"Last I knew, dirty dishes in the sink aren't a sin." Again she smiled.

Again he didn't.

Walking toward him, she stopped more than an arm's length away. "Why don't you go and take a nap?"

"At this hour of the morning?"

She shrugged as she took Heidi from him. "I've never heard there's a particular time for a nap. You're asleep on your feet."

"If I'm asleep, then why do I feel so tired?" He didn't try to halt another yawn.

"Maybe because you're on your feet. Go on, and get an hour or so of sleep. I'll keep the *kinder* as quiet as possible."

"I could sleep through an explosion."

"Go!" She motioned with her free hand. "Get some sleep."

He nodded, took a single step toward the front room

and the stairs, then asked, "So having you here today isn't a dream?"

He wanted to retract the words he'd meant to be a weak jest, but it was too late. The faint pink in Leanna's cheeks vanished as she whirled to pick up the scorched pan and put it on top of the other dishes in the sink. Muttering a *"danki"* under his breath, he strode out the door, letting the rusty screen slam in his wake.

How could he have spoken so foolishly? He couldn't blame it on his lack of sleep, because he'd guarded his words before. Maybe the sight of Leanna in his new home had torn down the walls he'd built around his battered heart the night he'd agree to marry Freda. Had seeing Leanna in his kitchen been enough to evoke the dreams he'd decimated when he stood before the *Leit* and vowed to be Freda's husband?

If so, he had to make sure it didn't happen again. He'd hurt her too much to risk doing so again. He must keep the boundaries in place between them.

Always.

Leanna flinched at the sound of a door closing upstairs a few minutes later. Gabriel must have come back in the front door so he could avoid her. Offering to help him until Juanita graduated from school had been a mistake.

A big mistake.

She had to find someone else to take her place. She shouldn't be here, because being around Gabriel brought too many futile hopes to life. He'd made his choice, and she had to accept that.

Her working at his house wasn't about her and about Gabriel. If it had been, she never would have volunteered to help him. The *bopplin* needed her to be there to feed them and change them and play with them.

And you need them.

The thought should have startled her, but it didn't. How often had she imagined having a family of her own? More than once, she'd thought about how much fun it would be to have twins so she could watch them grow up and grow close to each other as she and Annie had.

Harley and Heidi wouldn't be hers, but she could spend time with them in the years to come because they'd be part of the small community along Harmony Creek.

"How about something to eat?" she asked the little girl she held.

Heidi answered with nonsense sounds and grinned, dancing in Leanna's arms.

Seeing two high chairs set beside boxes waiting for someone to open them, she set the *boppli* on the blanket beside her brother. Leanna had moved one chair before she noticed Heidi crawling at a remarkable speed and intent toward the front room. Scooping up the *kind*, she put her in the high chair.

"You're a cute little monkey looking for trouble, ain't so?" Leanna made a silly face at the tiny girl.

"Be careful," replied a voice even deeper than Gabriel's. "Your face might freeze that way, and it'd be a shame."

Her eyes widened when she saw a dark-haired man standing in the doorway. He was taller than Gabriel, and his prominent nose would have dwarfed a face with gentler planes. Hints of red glistened in his hair when sunlight rippled across it.

"Gute mariye?" She hadn't intended to make the greeting a question, but she wasn't sure who the man was.

As if she'd asked that question, he said, "You must be Leanna. I'm Michael, the smarter twin."

Leanna smiled in spite of herself. She'd never met Gabriel's twin, and she was surprised how different the two men looked. Not just their coloring, but how Michael smiled easily while Gabriel remained somber even when she made a joke.

Gabriel used to laugh and smile. A lot. In fact, it had been his grin that first caught her eye during a Sunday evening gathering. He'd been on the opposite side of the barn, but when the enticing rumble of his laugh caught her ear, she had turned toward him. Her eyes had been captured by his dark brown ones, and a sensation she'd never known rushed through her like a rising wind before a thunderstorm. It was filled with warmth and anticipation and a hint of possible danger.

At the time, she'd been delighted by the instant connection between them. That had been before she'd come to understand the hint of danger was real and aimed at her heart.

"It's nice to meet you," she replied when Michael got the other high chair.

She set Harley in it and bent to tie a bib around the *boppli*'s neck.

"I hear you're a twin, too," Michael said as he leaned a shoulder against a cabinet.

"Ja."

"Are you the older or younger twin?"

"I'm sure I knew at one time or another. There are only five minutes between when we were born, so it doesn't matter."

Michael chuckled. "I guess twin girls aren't as competitive as male twins are. Gabriel never has let me forget he's almost an hour older than me. Of course, I tell him God gave him a head start because He knew Gabriel would need it to keep up with me."

Leanna laughed. As she motioned for Michael to help himself to a cup of *kaffi* while she cooked him and the *bopplin* some breakfast, she told him Gabriel was catching a quick nap.

"Gut," Michael replied. "He's a danger to himself and to everyone else if he tries to work when he can't keep his eyes open."

"Aren't the *bopplin* sleeping through the night?"

"Don't ask me. I wouldn't hear them if they came into my room and shrieked in my ears. Once I'm asleep, I don't hear anything." He opened the refrigerator and shifted the bottles before pulling out a pitcher of cows' *milch*. Pouring some into his cup, he grinned at her. "Sometimes, it's great to be oblivious."

She handed each of the *bopplin* a hard cookie to chew on, then went to the stove to crack some eggs into a fresh pan. She listened as Michael talked about the project the two brothers would be working on, and though it was a simple job, he sounded excited about doing it, especially the interior carpentry. He made jokes that had her laughing, though she tried to keep the sound low so she didn't wake Gabriel. She set a handful of fried-egg pieces on the trays of the two high chairs. She wasn't sure if the *kinder* would eat them, but the food would keep them entertained while she worked. When she put a plate with fried eggs and toast in front of Michael before returning to the stove to get bacon, he sat and dug in with the fervor of a man who hadn't eaten in a year.

"Slow down," she cautioned.

"Why? It's delicious."

"You two must not be very *gut* cooks, because I'm not. My sisters are the skilled cooks in our house."

He tapped his plate with his fork before scooping up

another piece of egg, "If your sisters are better cooks than this, point me to them. I'll propose today."

She laughed. "One is going to be married this fall, and the other is fourteen and still in school."

"I'll wait if her cooking is better than this." He gave her a wink, then reached for the strawberry jam to lather it on his toast.

Leanna walked to the stove. Gabriel's brother was charming.

As Gabriel used to be.

That thought sent a chilling wave of sorrow over her. She'd lost any chance to win Gabriel's heart, but it seemed Gabriel had lost himself since the last time she'd spoken to him in Lancaster County.

She couldn't think of anything sadder.

Chapter Five

Sitting on the floor beside Heidi and Harley, Leanna wiped first one *boppli*'s face, then the other's. She tried not to smile when they scrunched up their mouths, making it longer to get them clean. However, she'd learned to wash them quickly so they didn't have time to cry. Harley could turn on the tears within seconds, but Heidi seemed to suck in air for almost a minute before a cry of dismay or pain or anger burst out of her. The first time it had happened, it had taken all of Leanna's willpower not to laugh at the little girl's reaction to being told she couldn't crawl up the stairs.

In the two days since she'd started babysitting for Gabriel, she'd discovered Harley and Heidi were already developing personalities as divergent as hers and Annie's. Heidi was the more adventurous one. Harley could be kept content for hours playing with his fingers and toes. He didn't show any interest in exploring the floor and the stairs as his sister did. *Ja*, the *bopplin* were twins, but each of them was also his or her own person.

She gave in to her urge to grin as she thought of the many times people had assumed she and Annie were alike because they looked so similar. More than once she'd switched places with her sister at school when a distracted teacher gave them the opportunity.

Heidi flopped over to her stomach and pushed herself up to crawl again. Watching her, Leanna was amazed anew. The little girl's physical skills seemed too advanced for a six-month-old.

Grossmammi Inez's voice echoed in her mind, reminding her twins appeared younger than they were. Still, Heidi acted more advanced than she could possibly be.

Again Leanna counted on her fingers as she had several times already since she'd learned about the twins. No matter how she calculated, the twins had to be around six months old. Maybe a couple of weeks older. It seemed odd Heidi should be crawling and pulling herself up to stand.

"You're someone who can't wait, ain't so?" she asked as she picked up the *boppli* and cuddled her.

Heidi chuckled a deep belly laugh and squirmed with delight at the attention. She never acted upset when Leanna curtailed her explorations. Only when she was hungry did she lose her cheerful demeanor. Leanna had discovered that when she put the *bopplin* in their high chairs and didn't have something for Heidi to eat.

Sliding along the floor to where Heidi's brother was watching them and grinning, Leanna asked, "You're a bit more patient, ain't so? A bit."

Harley arched his back as if asking to be picked up, too, wriggling on the well-worn quilt on the floor. He already resembled his *daed* with his red hair, though his was more orange than Gabriel's.

Leanna set Heidi beside her, then bent over as she lifted Harley's white shirt, already covered with teething biscuit crumbs. She blew on his belly, and he gig-

gled. The sound was different from his sister's. Instead
of deep and joyful, it was more high-pitched. Each laugh
seemed to include a gulp at the end. If he were drawing
in that much air, he could end up with a tummy ache.

Raising her head, she murmured, "We don't want
that."

He held up his arms to her.

"Later," she promised as she stood. "I need to warm
up some bottles for two ravenous *bopplin*. Do you know
their names? I'll give you one hint. Their names start
with the letter *H*. Any guesses?"

She kept up a steady patter as she got two bottles
from the refrigerator and put them in a pot of hot water
to warm. She made a quick peanut butter sandwich for
herself. She found some potato chips, grateful again that
Gabriel had told her, after her first morning's arrival,
not to bring her lunch. He'd assured her he and Michael
preferred different foods so she should always be able
to find something she liked in the kitchen.

I have. You, her heart had wanted her to call out to
him as he'd turned to leave with his brother to go to
work.

She hadn't expected that her recalcitrant heart would
help her understand how impossible it was to control
her feelings. Had it been the same for Gabriel? Had he
walked out with her, hoping something would grow
between them, until his heart had demanded he heed
it and marry Freda?

Giving the bottles to the *bopplin* and making sure
they were settled on the quilt, Leanna ate her lunch. She
hadn't finished her sandwich before Heidi chucked her
empty bottle aside and pushed herself up to sit. A large
burp resonated through the kitchen.

"That sounds *gut*," Leanna said as she stooped to

pick up the discarded bottle. "How are you doing, Harley?"

She frowned when she noticed what appeared to be a bluish tint around his lips. She bent closer and scooped him up, holding him almost upright so he didn't drop the bottle. Examining him, she decided the light and shadows had deluded her, because his color appeared normal. She was being anxious when it was clear by how he was sucking on the bottle that he was fine.

Telling herself not to look for trouble, she cleaned up the *bopplin* and carried them upstairs. She no longer felt as ill at ease as she had the first day when she had wandered around Gabriel's house. It wasn't as if she were snooping.

Everything was scattered about, but that wasn't a surprise when the family had moved in a couple of weeks ago. Or maybe it was because the house was home to two single men and two *kinder*. She had to resist the temptation to put away the towels on a chair outside the bathroom door. Her arms were already full with the twins.

Both had to be changed, and she did that as soon as she reached their bedroom, which was big enough for two identical cribs, a changing table and a dresser. Once they were in fresh diapers and their faces clean again, she put them down for a nap.

Leanna headed downstairs. She glanced at her purse, hanging over a kitchen chair. A romance novel she was partway through was tucked inside, but as she took a single step into the kitchen any idea of reading a chapter or two while the *bopplin* slept vanished from her head.

Her sneaker stuck to something on the wood floor. Gabriel had said her job was only watching the *kinder*, but she couldn't stomach the idea of the *bopplin* crawling on such a dirty floor. Picking up the quilt, she put it on the bench by the table. She filled a bucket with soapy water and went to work on the kitchen floor. She was pleased to see it wasn't as dirty as she'd feared, though she found several other spots where someone must have dropped something sticky.

The floors in the other downstairs rooms were worse than she'd guessed. In the bathroom, the linoleum was so worn the pattern had vanished and brown spots showed through the top layer. It might once have been white or tan. The front room and the two bedrooms being used for storage sent her to the sink several times to dump out filthy water and get fresh.

Peering into the open boxes on the top of each pile, she saw a mishmash of household items and baby clothing. She hoped neither Gabriel nor Michael would be angry with her, but she began to unpack the boxes. She found places for dishes and cooking utensils in the kitchen, and put towels and washcloths in the bathrooms. Laundry supplies found a home on the wide shelves over the wringer washer.

Her next discovery was a pile of dirty clothing tall enough to reach her waist. She went into the laundry where more unpacked boxes waited. After checking that the washer was connected to water and a drain, she tossed in enough dark clothes to fill the tub. For the next two hours, she did laundry. She was glad to find a freestanding clothesline outside the laundry room door. Her shoulders and back ached from wringing out clothing, but she smiled when the clean items were flapping in the warm breeze.

By that time, the *bopplin* were awake and making sounds from their cribs. Leanna wasn't sure if they were calling to her or talking to each other. They chirped with excitement when she walked into the small bedroom. It had been the only room, other than the kitchen, not filled with unpacked boxes.

Had Gabriel and his brother been pulling out what they needed? It appeared that way, because she couldn't see any rhyme or reason to what had been unpacked. Though the *bopplin*'s small white room with its single window had no boxes, their clothing was piled on top of an overflowing dresser. She wondered why the tiny garments and diapers hadn't been put into the closet.

She got her answer when she lifted the old-fashioned latch to open the closet door. The narrow space was jammed from floor to ceiling with more boxes. Most were marked for the *bopplin*'s room, but she saw one labeled "kitchen" near the top.

"Lots more work to do, ain't so?" she asked the twins.

Before she could add more, the *bopplin* began to cry so loudly she wanted to put her hands over her ears. What was wrong? She rushed to the cribs, checking one and then the other. Neither needed to be changed, and it was way too early for their next bottles. She picked each of them up, trying to soothe them.

Nothing she did helped. Their cries rose to shrieks. Again she checked to make sure diaper pins hadn't come loose and were poking the twins. Were they suffering from teething pain? The biscuits were downstairs.

She bent to lift Harley out of his crib, then went to pick up Heidi. Balancing them, each tiny body stiff with fury, she turned toward the door.

Gabriel burst into the room. "Are you okay?"

Was he shouting to be heard over the *bopplin*'s screeching? She stared at his wild eyes as they scanned the room. She'd never seen him so upset.

Before she could reply, he said, "*Gut*. You're okay." His breath exploded out of him in relief, and his shoulders sagged as he put a hand on the door frame. "Thank the *gut* Lord."

Leanna bounced both *bopplin* as she asked, "Are *you* okay, Gabriel?"

He started to answer, then paused. While the *bopplin* continued to howl, he looked everywhere but at his *kinder* and her. "On the day Freda died, I came in and heard the twins crying. I called to her, and she didn't answer."

"You called to me today when you heard Harley and Heidi crying?"

He nodded.

If her arms hadn't been filled with *bopplin*, she wasn't sure she could have halted them from sweeping around him as she offered him comfort. She couldn't ease the pain of losing his wife, but she could show she understood how it felt to lose someone precious. When her parents had died, she'd learned pain loitered in her heart, ready to leap out at any moment. How much worse would it be to lose the *mamm* of your *kinder*?

Her tears blurred his strong face in front of her, and she bit her lower lip to keep her sob from slipping out. The tears fell, hot as acid along her cheek.

"May I?" he asked as he stepped toward her and raised his arm.

"*Ja*." She started to turn to hand him Heidi but froze when his fingers settled on her cheek, wiping away the tears.

The past seemed to reappear, taking them back to the night when she'd told him about how she was grateful to her *grossmammi* for sharing her small home with the orphaned Wagler siblings. She'd cried then, opening herself to him as she'd never done with anyone, and the first tendrils of love had emerged from her heart.

Leanna was pulled into the present when Michael shouted up the stairs to his brother. He needed help with some boards, and the urgency in his voice was clear.

"Go," she urged. "I've got these two."

"Leanna, I—" Gabriel choked on whatever he would have said next. Pushing off from the door, he strode away.

At the sound of his boots on the treads, she looked at the twins and forced a smile. "What am I going to do with you?"

She kept up a steady chatter of nonsense that seemed to break through the twins' distress. They calmed. She discovered they needed a diaper change and wondered if their stomachs had been bothering them. Deciding to be like the *bopplin* and forget they'd been crying a few minutes ago, she redressed them.

Yet she couldn't keep from thinking of how Gabriel's face had been shadowed by a panic she'd never thought she'd see there. Why hadn't she realized it was likely he'd been the one to discover Freda after her death? She wondered what other secrets he hid, secrets too appalling to bring into the light of day. Were those what she'd sensed? She couldn't ask, because she didn't want to risk seeing his haunted expression again.

Propping one twin on each hip, Leanna went down to the kitchen. Michael was sitting at the table, wiping a soiled kerchief against his sweaty forehead. Gabriel was about to sit as well when Leanna walked into the room. Jumping to his feet, Gabriel held out his hands toward her.

"Can I help?" he asked.

"I've got them." Squatting, she put one twin, then the

other, on the quilt she'd replaced on the floor. "Much easier when they're in a *gut* mood."

"You've got to teach him how to do that," Michael said with a laugh. "That way he won't have to depend on me."

"It just takes practice." Leanna stood and smoothed her apron over her skirt. "I learned how to handle more than one *boppli* when I helped with the younger *kinder* on Sundays."

"Show me?" Gabriel asked.

"Later." She motioned for him to sit beside his brother. He'd clearly decided to act as if their previous conversation hadn't happened, so she'd do the same. "I'll get you some lemonade."

"Lemonade?" His eyes widened. "I didn't know we had any mix in the house."

"It's freshly squeezed. I brought some lemons with me this morning."

"I told you that you didn't need to bring food with you," Gabriel said.

"Stop chiding her, and be grateful." His brother grinned. "You had time to do all that laundry hanging outside, make lemonade and take care of the *bopplin*? Are you sure there aren't three or four of you?"

"No," she replied with a laugh as she bent to pick up Harley. "Just two *bopplin* who took a longer nap than usual this afternoon."

Setting the little boy in one high chair, she smiled as Gabriel put Heidi in the other high chair. She tied bibs around the *bopplin* and handed each of them a teething biscuit before Heidi could begin wailing.

"Lemonade?" she asked.

Michael held up his hands. "*Danki*, but I'll have my lemonade without something to chew on." He hooked a thumb toward the *bopplin*, who were chewing on the biscuits.

His joking reminded her of how Gabriel used to do the same when they were walking out together, though expecting him now to be amusing when he was mourning his wife would be wrong.

Leanna filled three glasses and served one to each of the men before taking a sip out of her own. They downed them and she refilled their glasses, leaving the pitcher in the middle of the table.

After finishing his third glass, Michael stood. "I'll get the rest of those boards in the wagon, Gabriel, while you have some family time."

Gabriel nodded, and she wondered how much he'd told his brother about what had happened upstairs. Another question she must not ask.

Topping off his glass and her own, Gabriel looked at the crumb-covered twins, who were jabbering as they chewed on their biscuits. "They seem to understand each other."

"My *grossmammi* said Annie and I were talking to each other long before we invited others into our conversations." She lifted one shoulder in a casual shrug though she was too aware of each motion either she or Gabriel made, as well as any sound and aroma in the room. It was as if every sense was filled with as much anticipation as the *bopplin* had while waiting for their bottles. "*Grossmammi* Inez also said she believed, as twins, Annie and I used our own special language before we were born and just never stopped. We switched to *Deitsch* before we went to school."

"Do you know what your sister is thinking or feeling when she isn't nearby?"

"Sometimes." She wiped her hand on the dish towel,

then hung it up to dry. "I can do that with any of my siblings. It must come from living together and sharing so many experiences. Do you and Michael have more than a normal ability to do that?"

"I don't know what normal is, because he's my only sibling, though sometimes at work each of us knows what the other needs. People have asked if, as twins, we can read each other's thoughts. They seem to believe that's something all twins can do. I'm grateful it's not true for us."

He looked away, and she knew he'd come close to saying something he hadn't intended. About Freda or something else?

"How's the job going?" she asked, latching on to an innocuous subject.

"All right. Michael loves carpentry work. His plan is to focus on that while I get the farm up and running. He's never liked milking or working in the fields."

"So why did he come here?"

"Because we're his family," he replied as if that should explain it.

It did. Her younger siblings had been shocked at the abrupt announcement from their older brother, Lyndon, that they were moving to northern New York, but they hadn't quibbled. As for Leanna, she'd been excited to leave. She'd hoped being away from the past would help her forget what had happened since she'd heard Gabriel was marrying someone else.

Her gaze went to where Gabriel was lifting Heidi out of her chair and onto his lap. How could she have guessed her past would follow her? God must have planned for her to discover something by planting her past right on her doorstep, but what? To forgive? She should do that, but offering forgiveness without her heart being behind it was hypocrisy. God couldn't want her to do that, could He?

Do You? She aimed the prayer heavenward along with the hope she'd get an answer before she made the wrong decision.

Finally, with Leanna's help, Gabriel learned to balance one twin on each knee. Part of it was the twins were able to sit without help, though Harley kept a cautious handful of Gabriel's shirt gripped in his fingers. The rest was because he'd grown more confident in handling the *bopplin* each day.

As he watched Leanna warm bottles for the twins, her final task before she left for the day, he admired her easy efficiency. She had asserted several times she wasn't a *gut* cook, but she appeared to know her way around a kitchen. No motion was wasted, and her shoes didn't stick to the floor as his boots had that morning.

Looking down, he was surprised to see the wood gleaming in the sunlight. She must have mopped the floor. Not only the kitchen one, but the living room floor, too, he realized. His eyes widened. The stacks of boxes were gone. Only two remained.

"I hope you don't mind I unpacked some things while the *bopplin* were napping," Leanna said.

His eyes cut to where she stood by the sink wringing her apron.

"You didn't need to do that." He wasn't sure what else he should say, then added, "I appreciate what you did. Michael will, too. *Danki.*"

"I wasn't sure where some things go, so I left them in those two boxes. I knocked down the other boxes and put them in the laundry room. I hope that's okay."

"It's fine, but I don't expect you to clean the house on top of watching the twins."

Turning to the stove to lift out one bottle and testing the heat of the formula on her wrist, she said, "I'm glad to do it. I'm not used to sitting and doing nothing in the middle of the day." She lifted the pan and switched off the burner. She took out the bottles. Handing him one, she said, "Give Harley to me." Taking the little boy, she added, "It's your turn to be fed first, ain't it?" She looked at Gabriel, smiling. "There's no reason they can't be fed at the same time when we're both here."

"How did you convince Heidi to wait?" he asked as he tilted the little girl back in his arms and offered the bottle. She clamped her mouth on the nipple and put both hands on the bottle as if afraid he was going to snatch it away. "If I don't feed her first, she starts crying at a low level, but it quickly becomes a shriek."

"I give them their bottles lying on the quilt."

"I never thought of doing that."

"They're big enough to hold their own bottles, but if I end up giving Harley his first and I don't want Heidi to be upset, I talk to her."

"Talk?"

She smiled as she sat on the bench facing him. "*Ja*, talk. I'm finding Heidi can be distracted from what she believes is her due if she's diverted by talk or a toy."

"That has never worked for me."

"So far it has for me, but it may be because I'm someone new and different. Once she gets accustomed to me, she may not be so willing to be diverted."

"They seem to be doing well with the goats' *milch*." He watched Heidi drinking the formula almost as fast as he had his first glass of Leanna's delicious lemonade.

"They can be weaned onto soy *milch* or almond *milch*, but they may never be able to drink cows' *milch*."

"Imagine that. A dairy farm whose *kinder* can't drink his *milch*."

"You wouldn't be the first. Or the last."

"True." He shifted the little girl in his arms, which were beginning to ache from his long hours of nailing over his head. "Your *grossmammi* mentioned you sell your soap at the farmers market in Salem."

"I did last year, and I've been planning to this year. Each day when I milk my goats, I set aside a small portion of the *milch* to make soap. I have almost enough for another batch, which I'll sell later in the summer. The soap I'll be selling when the farmers market opens is already made up. I need to wrap the bars, so they won't stick together when the sun's heat is on them."

"I'm surprised."

"That I make soap?"

"*Ja*, a bit. I thought you'd sell your quilts. You used to talk about quilting a lot."

She shrugged, and he wondered if he'd upset her with his comments about the past. No hint of that tainted her voice as she replied, "People coming to a farmers market are looking for small things because most of them have walked there. They don't want to tote a big quilt home. Besides, I can sell any quilted articles I make at Caleb's bakery."

"That's the one out of the main road?"

"*Ja*. He's taken some of my items on consignment. Even there, small table runners and wall hangings sell better than a full-size quilt."

"You've stopped making big quilts?"

She shook her head. "No, I recently finished one that a lady at the fire department's mud sale asked me to make for her. She'd bid on the one I donated, but didn't win it, so I agreed to make her a similar one for the cost of the materials if she'd donate the difference to the fire department."

Gabriel nodded, knowing he shouldn't be surprised. Leanna wouldn't think twice about making such an offer when it would help someone else.

He was sorry when Heidi finished her bottle, followed by Harley. Leanna rinsed them out and put them in her cloth bag to take home so she could refill them with formula.

Setting the bag on the table, she said, "I left a casserole in the oven for your supper." She paused as she reached for her bonnet. "Don't worry. I didn't cook it. Annie made two for us last night, and she asked me to bring it over here for you."

"*Danki.* I don't know what we would have done without—"

"Neighbors help neighbors," she replied primly.

Had he insulted her? Everything he said, no matter how well-intentioned, came out wrong. But it also seemed wrong not to acknowledge how the Waglers had gone beyond neighborly and had taken on the burden of looking after the Miller family. He understood no thanks were expected, but he also didn't like the idea of being indebted to them when he'd brought so much pain to Leanna and, through her, to her whole family.

There were many things he wanted to say to her, but he had to content himself with, "I wanted you to know Michael and I really appreciate your help."

"I'll pass your thanks on to Annie and *Grossmammi* Inez."

"*Danki,*" he said again, though he wanted to ask why she wasn't accepting some of his gratitude for herself.

The answer blared into his head when the door closed behind her, leaving him alone with the twins. To acknowledge his appreciation would risk re-creating an emotional connection between them, one he'd thought would last a lifetime. She wasn't ready to take that chance again, and he shouldn't be, either.

So why had images of them walking together or riding in his courting buggy never stopped filling his mind during the day and his dreams every night?

Chapter Six

The village of West Rupert was so small it barely deserved the name. A dozen houses spread along the narrow road, a white church set next to a cemetery, a fire station and a general store with antlers mounted over the door comprised the whole village. Small farms edged the roads leading in and out of town. The fields were sloped on one side and flat along a meandering stream on the other. The road continuing to the east led over Rupert Mountain and to the ski resorts along the spine of the Green Mountains.

Gabriel balanced on the top of a ladder leaning against what he guessed had originally been a storage barn for *milch* cans. Looking past the rafters he and Michael would finish rebuilding this morning, he stared at the meandering creek. It either was the same one or connected with the creek that ran through Harmony Creek Hollow and on down into the center of Salem.

His mind went with the water toward the fields he'd be planting next year. The mountains that rose around him were so different from the rolling hills where he'd grown up in Pennsylvania. The background to his days had changed in as spectacular way as his life had. He and Michael now owned a farm, and he had a family to raise there.

And Leanna was in his home, watching over his *kinder* as if she were their *mamm*. A double pulse of regret surged through him. Freda should have been the one tending to her twins. Leanna should never have been hurt by the promise he'd made to Aden. He wasn't sure which situation he rued more.

He was grateful Leanna had gone along with his intention of ignoring what had happened when he'd panicked at the *bopplin* crying so hard and nobody answering when he called out. If she'd asked questions about the day he'd come home to learn Freda was dead, he wasn't sure if he could have withheld the whole truth.

About how Freda had given in to her depression and committed suicide. About how he had failed to notice she was suffering from more than what she'd assured him were "*boppli* blues."

How, God, did I miss the signs right in front of me? Why did You let her suffer when I could have helped if You'd opened my eyes and my heart to what she needed?

Those questions had raged through him from the moment he realized Freda wasn't asleep, that the empty pill bottles had taken her away from the *kinder* he'd believed she loved too much to abandon. He wished they could have found the love a man and wife should have, but she'd been inconsolable from the moment her *Englischer* turned from her. The *Englischer* whose photo was beside her on the bed the day she died. She'd accepted Gabriel's offer of marriage and never asked for more, because she had given her heart to another.

As you did.

He closed his eyes, wishing he could reach out to God in something other than frustration and anger.

"Hey, are you asleep up there?" called Michael from the base of the ladder.

"Waiting on you to stop wandering around and get to work." He was grateful to be able to tease his brother, letting Michael's laughter sweep away his dreary thoughts.

"I'm here. Let's get going." He hefted a board up along the side of the garage, where any hint of paint had vanished years ago.

Gabriel grabbed the top and guided it to where he could put it in place. He aimed his hammer at the nail at the end of the board. With a pair of quick swings, he drove that nail and another in to hold the two sides of a rafter together. He appraised how the final rafter aligned with the others.

"Looking straight," Michael shouted.

"It should." Gabriel descended the ladder, glad Michael kept one hand on it. "You measured it over and over before cutting the angle."

"I wanted to make sure it was right when there will be two skylights in the roof."

"Making those calculations are something we can do in our sleep."

"Maybe I can, but when's the last time you slept through the night? I heard you pacing last night. What's going on?" He gave a terse laugh and answered before Gabriel could. "It's her, ain't so? Having Leanna at the house every day has you agog."

"I wouldn't say that," he hedged.

"Then what would you say?"

Gabriel was spared from answering when the homeowner, an *Englischer* named Don Fenton who planned to turn the building into an art studio for his wife, walked toward them. Talking to Don wasn't easy because the *Englischer* knew less about carpentry than Gabriel knew about sending a man to the moon. While Gabriel explained what they were doing—and why—his brother went to the stack of lumber.

Mrs. Fenton wandered out and began asking about flower boxes on the three windows the gray-haired lady wanted on each side. Gabriel listened and made a few suggestions, though it was the first time he'd heard about flower boxes. Maybe she'd mentioned them to Michael, and his brother had forgotten to say anything. No, that wasn't likely. Michael wrote down every detail of a project in the notebook he shared each night with Gabriel. Nothing had been in there about flower boxes.

It wasn't a problem. They could use a few pieces of leftover wood to make what she was looking for.

"Are you going to bring your twins here one of these days?" Mrs. Fenton asked, startling him out of his thoughts.

"Not while work is going on." He tried to keep his voice upbeat, but the beginnings of a headache was building between his eyebrows. "Too many things here are too dangerous for little ones."

She laughed. "I understand. When my children were small, they could find trouble where there shouldn't have been any. I do hope you and your brother will bring the babies and join us when we inaugurate my new studio."

"Of course." What else could he say? A party for a storage barn getting a new roof, windows and paint? Sometimes he found *Englischers* incomprehensible.

Gabriel talked for a few minutes more with the Fentons, then returned to work. His brother had estimated it would take them a month to complete the repairs and paint the building inside and out, but they might be finished sooner than that, so he and Michael needed to look for more jobs. Whether they worked together on the project or took two separate ones, he knew the money they'd make on this job wouldn't last long.

By the time the sun was high in the sky, Gabriel was ready to eat. He washed his hands with a hose attached to the main house before joining his brother, who sat at a nearby picnic table. They bowed their heads in silent thanks before reaching for the tuna sandwiches Michael had made that morning while Gabriel was giving the twins their morning bottles.

Gabriel's first bite warned him his brother had added too much mayonnaise. He tried not to grimace, but Michael did and put the sandwich down.

"That's disgusting," his twin said. "You shouldn't let me make lunch."

"I told you I'd do it." Gabriel took a huge bite of his own sandwich, swallowing it almost whole so he didn't have to taste it.

"And when would you have had the time?"

"I could get up earlier."

Michael's frown deepened. "You're half-asleep on your feet most of the time. Maybe you need to rethink Leanna's *grossmammi*'s offer to send over food for us."

"They're doing enough for us already."

Standing, Michael grabbed a handful of pretzels and his thermos of iced tea. "We need help. You might thrive on stress and drama—"

"I despise it."

"For someone who despises drama, you sure seem to surround yourself with it."

Gabriel's fingers clenched on his sandwich. Forcing them to ease off their death grip, he scowled at the mayo oozing around his fingers. He reached for a cloth to wipe his hands before saying, "Because lots of things have happened doesn't mean I wanted any of them to happen."

His brother's face fell, and he looked stricken. "I didn't mean… I wasn't talking about Freda dying."

"I know." He kneaded his forehead where the small headache was becoming the thunder of stampeding horses.

"I was talking about Leanna Wagler."

"I know," he said, wondering why his brother was stating the obvious.

"Has she said anything?"

He gave a humorless snort. "She's said a lot."

"You know what I mean. You spent hours working on that letter you sent her, and you never got an answer. Has she explained why?"

Standing, Gabriel stuffed his unfinished sandwich into the plastic lunch box they shared. "She doesn't owe me any explanation."

"There you go again. Drama." Michael sighed. "At least it won't be forever. Her sister graduates soon. It'll be different when Juanita is watching the twins."

"You're right."

He *hoped* his brother was correct. Though Leanna wouldn't be at their house each day, she'd be next door. How was he supposed to ignore her when his heart kept reminding him of the dreams it once had harbored? Once? With a silent groan, he knew those dreams of having her as his wife and the *mamm* of his *kinder* hadn't vanished.

Leanna glanced from the road to her *grossmammi*, who sat on the passenger side of the family's gray-topped buggy. *Grossmammi* Inez was staring straight ahead. Her lips moved, but no sound emerged. Guessing the older woman was praying, Leanna added a few silent pleas of her own.

The appointment with the cardiologist, who came one day every other week to the medical offices in Salem, hadn't gone the way either of them had hoped. Leanna knew her *grossmammi* hadn't really believed her shortness of breath had anything to do with the last winter's cold, but *Grossmammi* Inez hadn't expected to hear there was a problem with her heart.

Leanna had listened to the *doktor* explain in simple terms how one of her *grossmammi*'s heart valves had become constricted, making it impossible for her heart to get enough oxygen into her blood.

Tests would confirm the *doktor*'s diagnosis, so another appointment was made to confer with the cardiologist after those were done. The office had told Leanna to check in at week's end to find out when those tests could be run, and had alerted her that *Grossmammi* Inez would need to travel to the clinic—almost thirty miles away—for the tests.

That meant contacting Hank Puente, who made his large, white van available to the plain community. The short, jovial man was retired, and Leanna guessed he enjoyed the company of his neighbors more than the small amount he charged to drive them to places too far to go in a buggy. Once she had the day and time of the appointment, she'd have her twin sister call Hank from the phone in Caleb's bakery.

That part was easy.

What wasn't was knowing something was wrong with her *grossmammi*'s heart. She'd realized *Grossmammi* Inez's gasping for breath meant something wasn't right, but right up until the moment the cardiologist started explaining his findings, Leanna had hoped it was something simple. Something that could be healed with a round of antibiotics.

More than once during the half-hour ride from the village, Leanna thought about starting a conversation to break the silence. Each time she'd halted herself.

She sighed with relief when she drove into the Waglers' dooryard and stopped the buggy. Jumping out, she considered walking around it to help her *grossmammi*. Again she stopped herself. *Grossmammi* Inez had refused her assistance to get into the buggy at the *doktor*'s office, announcing loudly enough for everyone on the street to hear that she wasn't an invalid.

Leanna delayed unhitching the horse and walked with the older woman toward the house. When *Grossmammi* Inez held on to the railing along the steps, Leanna's breath caught in her throat. The motion warned her *grossmammi* might be suffering more than Leanna had guessed.

Inside the house, her siblings, including Lyndon with his family, were waiting. School was out, and it was, Leanna was shocked to realize, long past time for supper. The appointment had been late in the day, and she and *Grossmammi* Inez had sat in the waiting room for over an hour waiting to see the cardiologist.

The receptionist had suggested Leanna take an appointment early in the morning, but Leanna had made today's so she could work her regular hours at the Millers' house. Gabriel had been pleased he wouldn't miss much time at work. She wondered what he'd say when she told him she'd need time to take her *grossmammi* for testing.

A pang cut through her when she realized that by the time the testing was scheduled, she might no longer be watching the Miller twins. Juanita would have taken over the job by then, and Leanna would return to cleaning houses. All too soon she wouldn't be spending each day with those adorable *bopplin*.

Until supper was on the table and silent grace had given them time to thank God for the food and family with them, nobody asked a single question about the visit with the cardiologist. The pot of Annie's delicious beef stew and platters of buttermilk biscuits were passed around, and still nobody spoke.

Leanna's eyes were caught by her twin's, and she saw her dismay reflected in Annie's blue eyes. She mouthed the word *later* before taking a bite of stew. She chewed and chewed, but found it impossible to swallow. She noticed the only one eating was her *grossmammi*. Even Lyndon's young *kinder* seemed too antsy to do more than nibble at their biscuits, getting more crumbs down the front of them than into their mouths.

Grossmammi Inez glanced around the table. "You might as well spit out what you've got to say. Maybe then you can eat your supper."

Questions came from around the table. Leanna listened while their *grossmammi* answered with a reassuring smile. When the elderly woman paused between every word to gasp for breath, her family's worried expressions deepened.

"Don't look so upset," *Grossmammi* Inez said with an uneven laugh. "Remember the *doktor* said I might be able to take pills to help me." She didn't look in Leanna's direction. "Let's get that peach pie Annie brought from the bakery. Juanita, glasses of *milch* all around would be *wunderbaar*."

While her twin went to slice the pie, Leanna followed. She whispered a quick overview of what their *grossmammi* had omitted from what the cardiologist had said. Leanna saw more questions in her sister's eyes. Those would have to wait until after *Grossmammi* Inez went to bed.

They ate their dessert, which Leanna assumed was delicious because everything from the bakery was, whether Annie or Caleb made it. Tonight, the pie was tasteless. That Kenny didn't ask for seconds showed he was pretending as much as she was that everything was normal. Her younger brother loved peach pie and always had a second—and sometimes a third—slice.

Instead of lingering over their meal to chat about their day, everyone was up as soon as they'd finished. *Grossmammi* Inez excused herself and headed to bed, exhausted from the day. Lyndon herded his family out, and the kitchen grew silent.

Ten minutes later, draping the damp dish towel over the last of the dishes set in the drainer, Leanna joined her siblings in the front room. She sat next to Kenny on the light brown couch. That allowed her to face Annie who was rocking by the unlit woodstove. Juanita perched on the edge of a footstool in front of the chair where *Grossmammi* Inez used to sit and read the Bible aloud to them. The older woman had stopped when talking became too difficult.

"Tell us," Annie said.

"The *doktor* acted as if this condition wasn't anything unusual for a woman her age," Leanna said, taking care not to use her *grossmammi*'s name. She doubted their lowered voices would wake *Grossmammi* Inez, but she didn't want to take any chances.

"So it's possible taking pills could solve the problem?" asked Kenny, looking younger than his twelve years.

Leanna put her arm around his quaking shoulders.

He was struggling not to cry. Sometimes, because he matched their older brother step for step working on the farm, she forgot he was still a *kind*.

"We have to wait and see what the tests reveal," she said, giving him a squeeze. "While we wait, we need to pray for God to guide the *doktors* so they can help *Grossmammi* Inez."

When her siblings rose to seek their own beds, because they'd be up with the sun in the morning, Leanna didn't follow them toward the stairs.

"I'll be up in a minute," she said. "I want to make sure the goats don't get out. There have been sightings of coyotes around the area, and the kids could be vulnerable."

Annie gave her a taut smile. "Sleep well."

"I'll try. You, too."

By the time Leanna had checked her goats and returned to the house, she was too restless to sleep. She poured herself a glass of water and walked onto the front porch. As she sat on a rocker that had little of its original green paint, the mountains to the west were backlit by a flicker of lightning. The dull rumble of distant thunder faded away. Overhead stars glittered, but clouds gobbled up a few as she watched.

"Leanna?" came a voice from the darkness closer to the ground.

She gave a soft cry as she almost jumped out of the chair.

Gabriel stepped into the dim light shining from the living room. "I'm sorry. I didn't mean to startle you. I figured you'd heard me coming up the walk."

"I was watching the storm. Lost in thought." Her voice sounded as breathless in her ears as *Grossmammi* Inez's did.

"I wanted to find out how Inez's appointment went."

She knew she should invite him to come up on the porch and sit, but the words wouldn't form. Then she told herself she was silly. What had happened had happened, and she couldn't change it. She motioned for him to take the chair beside hers.

When he had, she stared again at the sky. It was easier than looking at him. If she saw sorrow on his face, she might lose her grip on her emotions. She didn't want to break down in front of him.

"The appointment went as well as can be expected," she said after explaining what the *doktor* suspected was wrong. "They want to run a few tests to confirm the diagnosis, and then they'll decide what to do."

"When are they doing the tests?"

"Soon. I'm supposed to check in at week's end to find out when they've scheduled her to come in."

He frowned. "They don't seem to be in any hurry."

"I know, but I have to accept they know what they're doing. They deal with patients all day long."

"But this patient is your *grossmammi*." A gentle compassion eased into his voice.

"Ja." She wrapped her arms around herself. To ward off the cold the thought of surgery sent through her? Or to halt the warmth surging forth at his heartfelt words? She didn't want to delve too deeply. "And I can't help worrying the process is going on too long. On the other hand, if there's a way she can avoid surgery, the delay will be worth it. The *doktor* said some people can be treated by taking a pill. It depends on what the tests show. We have to trust in God's plan."

He gave a rude snort, shocking her as much as his arrival had. "God's plan?"

"You don't believe God has a plan for each of us?"

"Oh, I'm sure He has a plan." His voice hardened. "I'm also sure it doesn't have anything to do with what we want or need."

Leanna bit her lower lip as she heard the pain he couldn't conceal. Not so long ago, he'd buried his wife and her *daed*, a man who'd raised Gabriel and his twin as if they were his own sons. He'd been left to raise his *kinder* without a *mamm*, something he'd experienced himself so he knew about the void that would leave in the *bopplin*'s hearts.

Sympathy for him and his family threatened to overwhelm her. She didn't want to dim what happiness he had left.

A smile tilted her lips. She had just the way!

"I have something to show you." She stood. "Wait here."

"What have you got to show me?"

She smiled. "I've always heard patience is a virtue."

"I've heard that, too." He cocked an eyebrow at her. "I'm not sure I believe it, because satisfying my curiosity is always a blessing."

Leanna almost gasped. Had Gabriel made a jest? If so, it was the first time she'd heard him do so since the last time they'd walked out together. Maybe he hadn't changed as much as she'd believed.

Alarms sounded through her head. If he hadn't changed into the dour man he'd acted, then the danger to her heart was greater than she'd guessed. She'd fallen in love with the amusing man he'd been in Lancaster County.

So had Freda Girod.

She rushed into the house before her face revealed what she was thinking. A moment later, she wheeled a small red wagon onto the porch. "I thought you could use this to pull the *kinder* around in. That way, you don't have to try to carry both by yourself if nobody else can help you."

"They're young to ride in a wagon," he said as he came to his feet. Surprise widened his eyes when he looked from the wagon to her.

"That's why I had Lyndon put these wooden insets on each side." She ran her fingers along the panels that were about six inches high and encircled the wagon.

He knelt to examine them. "I've seen wagons like this before. I always wondered what the slits were in the sides."

"The boards will keep Harley and Heidi from tumbling out."

"And Heidi from climbing out."

She shook her head. "I'm not so sure about that. I'm beginning to think your little girl is planning to be a mountain climber when she grows up. If she waits that long."

"This is remarkable, Leanna." He stood, and for a second she thought he was going to smile.

It must have been a trick of the poor light. Telling herself she should be grateful he hadn't smiled, because she was unsure she could resist that, she replied, "I remembered we had a little wagon for Kenny when he was a *boppli.* I found this one at the thrift store by the old courthouse and cleaned it. I think it'll make it easier for them to go for an outing."

"You never said anything about it."

"I wasn't sure when Lyndon would be able to get around to building the panels."

He arched an eyebrow at her. "My brother is a carpenter. Remember?"

"I know, but it might not have been a surprise if I'd asked him."

"Michael is pretty *gut* at keeping secrets."

For a moment, she was tempted to ask if Michael was as skilled at hiding things as Gabriel was. She didn't say anything because that would ruin the simple happiness of being able to present him with this gift from the whole Wagler family.

"Well," she said, "now he can be surprised, too."

"I'm overwhelmed." He put his fingers on her arm. "*Danki*. The *bopplin* will love it, I'm sure."

"*Gut.*" She edged away so the buzz emanating from the spot where his skin touched hers eased and allowed her to think. "And *danki* for stopping by. I'll let *Grossmammi* Inez know you called."

He stared at her for so long she wondered if he'd turned into a statue. He started to speak once, then a second time. Finally he said, as he picked up the wagon, "*Gut nacht,* Leanna. *Danki* again."

"*Gut nacht,*" she replied, resting her hand on the porch support as she watched him walk down the steps and disappear into the darkness.

Thunder rolled, much nearer than it had been before. She was astonished she hadn't noticed how the storm was approaching. Lost in the wonder of Gabriel's touch, chaste though it'd been, had made her unaware of everything else. What would have happened if she hadn't stepped aside when he'd brushed his fingertips on her arm? If she'd, instead, moved closer?

She let her head loll against the porch column as lightning sewed a brilliant seam between the clouds. She had done the right thing to protect her heart from being hammered again, so why did she feel so lousy?

Chapter Seven

Sunday dawned with the promise of a lovely day to come. The sunrise painted the eastern sky with astounding colors that couldn't be found in a box of crayons. Spring kept the air a bit crisp and lighter than it would be when the middle of summer battered them with heat and humidity.

Leanna finished pinning up her hair and set her *kapp* in place before going to stand by the single window in her bedroom. Looking down at her goats, who were gathered near the gate as they waited for her to come to feed, water and milk them, she smiled. She was glad the services in Harmony Creek Hollow were close to their house so the family could stay to enjoy the company of the other members of the *Leit* before evening chores.

The Sabbath was set aside as a day of rest except for tending to their animals. No cooking or baking or housework allowed. Only the necessary tasks of taking care of those who couldn't take care of themselves. Leanna wrapped her arms around herself as she thought of how they'd be allowed to nurse *Grossmammi* Inez on a Sunday. No, she didn't want to think of a time when her *grossmammi* couldn't manage simple tasks on her own.

Nobody else was downstairs when she returned from milking her goats. She'd heard voices from the main barn, so she knew Lyndon and Kenny were milking. What a blessing it was her younger brother could do everything he had before that accident during the winter! He'd healed but not fast enough for an impatient boy who'd been hit by a skidding car while he was skiing behind a fast-moving buggy along a snowy road. She hoped he'd be less of a risk-taker the next time he and his friends got such a ridiculous idea in their heads.

Leanna put the fresh *milch* in the refrigerator on the far right side. That would keep it separated from the *milch* Kenny brought from the cow barn. She had to shift a few of the *bopplin*'s bottles to find room for her metal *milch* container. Yesterday *Grossmammi* Inez had made a double batch of formula for the Miller twins, so they didn't have to prepare any today. Later she would put the leftover *milch* into the freezer. It should give her enough to make up a batch of soap for the farmers market.

Ignoring the dread bubbling up in her as she thought about having to talk to strangers who were interested in her soap, she focused instead on filling cups with the *kaffi* Annie had prepared. Her *grossmammi* and her siblings drank as if they'd crawled across a desert. Biscuits left from last night's supper were topped with different types of butter, including apple and peanut.

Church was being held at the Bowmans' farm, which was closer to the main road that ran from Salem to the Vermont state line. *Grossmammi* Magdalena, who oversaw the Bowman household, had held a work frolic earlier in the week to make sure everything was ready for the service and the *Leit*. As it'd been held during the Miller *bopplin*'s nap time, Leanna hadn't taken part. However, she knew the Bowman farm well because they'd held services there a couple of times already. The number of households in Harmony Creek Hollow was small, so each family hosted church more often than in bigger districts. No one minded, because it was an honor to provide space for the *Leit* to worship together.

Though the house was a short distance away, Leanna and Annie insisted on taking the buggy. It was too far for *Grossmammi* Inez to walk. Lyndon's younger *kinder* rode with them, excited to have a chance to spend time with their beloved great-*grossmammi*. The rest would walk.

The Bowmans' house was the smallest one in Harmony Creek Hollow, so the service would be held in a barn. The double doors had been thrown open wide, and the sun shone in to banish the shadows to the deepest corners. Benches had been put in place, two sets so the men could face the women during the service. Tarps beneath them would protect clothing from grit left by years of driving farm vehicles in and out.

Grossmammi Inez went to join the other older women who had gathered in the shade of a pair of huge maple trees. Annie and Leanna watched while their brother's *kinder* skipped across the grass to join their *mamm*. When Annie said she'd be right back, Leanna wasn't surprised she walked at a much more sedate pace toward where Caleb Hartz was getting out of his buggy. Nobody would be surprised when the two published their plans to marry in the fall.

Turning to join the other women, Leanna couldn't keep her eyes from focusing on Gabriel, who held the handle of the wagon she'd given him. His bright red hair was hidden beneath the black church hat that matched the *mutze* coat and trousers he wore. Her breath caught against her pounding heart when she noticed how broad his shoulders appeared.

He looked in her direction, and their gazes collided. It was almost a physical impact, and she was surprised she wasn't rocked back on her heels. Her breath stuck over her heart, which seemed to be trying to break a speed record. Its thud hammered like a cloudburst in her ears.

Leanna dropped her gaze, hoping her face hadn't displayed—in that ever so brief second—how her heart hadn't changed in spite of his choosing another over her. She walked past a group of twittering teenage girls and ignored their speculation about which of the available *maedels* Gabriel should consider as a wife. Her name wasn't mentioned, and she tried not to let that bother her. Though she'd never guessed when her sister and their friends started the Harmony Creek Spinsters Club that a year later she'd be the only one with no plans to marry.

Shaking her head, she kept walking. She would marry if—and only if—God's plan for her included marriage. As she tried to talk sense to her aching heart, she wondered if Gabriel realized how much talk there was among the unmarried women about his need for a wife.

He did, she discovered, when instead of handing off the twins to sit with the women and other small *kinder*, he kept both *bopplin* with him while he sat next to his brother on the men's side. She wasn't surprised when Gabriel got up twice and Michael once more with the *bopplin* when they became fussy or needed to be changed during the three-hour service. Though it was unusual for a *daed* or *onkel* to handle such chores, she knew Gabriel had been wise not to ask any of the women to take care of his *kinder*. Such a request would have been seen as a possible invitation to become better acquainted.

She fixed her mind on the service, but her eyes kept shifting toward Gabriel. It was startling to realize they'd never worshipped together before this. They'd spent hours talking about everything, including their faith, during the time they'd walked out together.

At the end of the service, Leanna rose and joined the other women getting the cold sandwiches and preserves waiting in the kitchen. The men shifted the benches to make tables for the meal the *Leit* would share. As always, the oldest men moved to the table first.

Leanna emerged from the house with a platter of sandwiches and set them on one end of the table. She was about to go for another plate when she saw Gabriel pull the wagon up to the table and heard a wail from it.

Heidi!

Moving to where Gabriel was trying to calm the little girl, Leanna said, "I'll watch them while you eat."

"You don't have to do that. We can—"

Michael interrupted, "*Danki*, Leanna. I, for one, appreciate your offer." He aimed a steady look at his brother. "That's true, ain't so, Gabriel? No need for any *drama* today, ain't so?"

What was exchanged between the twin brothers was beyond Leanna's comprehension, but she was sure she'd heard the slightest emphasis when Michael said *drama*. That meant something to the brothers, and she doubted Gabriel would want her probing into what was going on.

Leanna picked up Heidi and crooned, "There, there. So much noise from such a tiny mouth. What's going on with you, *boppli*?"

The *kind*'s face softened from its scowl, and she began to gurgle. Relief eased the lines in Gabriel's brow.

"I owe you one," Gabriel said.

"Nonsense." Leanna cuddled the little girl and tickled her belly. "I'm glad to help."

"I know you are, but I still owe you one."

Michael chuckled. "Don't bother to argue, Leanna. I learned years ago it's a waste of breath. Let him owe you one. And don't worry about him forgetting it. Gabriel always keeps his promises." He winked at his brother. "That's one thing you can count on. Once Gabriel Miller says he's going to do something, he does it. That's right, ain't so?"

Gabriel's shoulders stiffened as he'd been about to reach for his son. "I guess so."

Leanna glanced from one brother to the other. Again some message she wasn't privy to had passed between them, but she wasn't sure which of Michael's words bothered Gabriel. It had to be more than his brother complimenting him.

Gabriel mumbled something that she guessed was *"Danki."* To his brother or to her?

Gathering up Harley after Michael walked away to speak with their minister, Eli Troyer, she said, "Gabriel, there's a question I've been meaning to ask you."

"Go ahead."

"Are you okay with me taking the *bopplin* off your farm while I'm watching them?"

"Of course." His familiar frown returned. "Why would you ask such a thing? Don't you think I trust you?"

"No, that's not it. I know you trust me. You wouldn't have asked me to watch your *kinder* if you didn't trust me." She edged away one step, then another. "You're their *daed*, and I thought I should check with you before I do anything different with them."

She sounded like a *dummkopf*, babbling as if she

couldn't stop. She clamped her mouth closed before she said something she'd regret for the rest of her life.

When Leanna looked away, Gabriel understood what she was trying to avoid saying. It wasn't a matter of him trusting her. It was about her not trusting *him*. And why should she? He'd betrayed her once.

At least that was how she must see it.

It was how *anyone* would see the events that had occurred. If he could be honest with her, maybe she would have forgiven him. He rued the letter he'd written, because it must have seemed ridiculous to her when he couldn't explain the truth of why he'd agreed to Freda's *daed*'s proposition. Knowing how Leanna cared for her own family, he guessed she might have forgiven him if he'd been able to tell her why he'd stood her up and married someone else such a short time later.

The truth burned on his lips, begging to be spoken. How many times had Aden reminded him, Michael and Freda that the truth would set them free? He'd told them being honest kept them from being bound by ropes of lies that would grow tighter with each layer added.

So why, Aden, did you bind me to a promise that keeps me from being honest with Leanna?

"Where do you want to take the *bopplin*?" Gabriel asked.

"I thought they might like to visit my goats."

"That's not dangerous?"

"Do you think I'd do something to put the twins in danger?" Her blue-green eyes snapped, and he knew he'd upset her again.

He wasn't sure why he kept doing things to distress her. Was keeping a chasm between them a way to prevent him from having to think about what they'd shared in the past? If so, it wasn't working.

"No, of course not. I know you love Heidi and Harley. But I know these two *kinder*. I know they will go looking for trouble whenever possible. Or at least Heidi will."

"She's curious about things. Like her *daed*." Her smile for the *bopplin* was warm, and it widened to include him, as well.

He couldn't smile because her words were a slap in the face. A reminder of the truth he wished he could share with her and close the chasm between them.

He couldn't let that happen. He'd failed as a husband once. He couldn't risk doing that again.

Monday evening, Gabriel came home to an empty house. He found a note in the middle of the kitchen table. It was from Leanna and told him she and the *bopplin* were at her family's farm. She asked him and Michael to meet them there for supper.

He handed the note to his brother before heading into the bathroom for a quick shower. Tomorrow he and Michael would paint the Fentons' art studio, so they'd spent the day smoothing joint compound on the new walls. A glance in the mirror as he waited for the water to warm up showed how much plaster dust covered him. Now he knew what he'd look like when his hair and beard were more white than red. He rushed through his shower. Coming back into the kitchen, he let Michael know it was his turn to clean up.

"I'm heading next door to get the twins, " he said as he reached for his hat.

"In a hurry to see our pretty neighbor?" asked Michael, dropping his suspenders over his shoulders as he walked toward the bathroom.

"*Ja.*"

The honest answer surprised his brother, halting him as he was about to close the bathroom door. Gabriel didn't blame his brother.

It didn't take Gabriel long to find Leanna and the twins at the Wagler farm. She'd told him she wanted to bring the *bopplin* to meet her goats. Going to the pen where the animals were kept, he held his breath, not wanting to interrupt the scene in front of him.

Leanna sat on the box where she milked her goats. Heidi was perched on Leanna's knee and bounced with excitement while Harley sat in the wagon, staring with big eyes at the goats, which must seem huge to such a tiny boy. Heidi's fingers were outstretched and wiggled as if she could lure the goats to her with the motion.

Leanna made a soft, clicking sound, and the goats looked toward her, their ears up. One brown-and-white goat edged forward. It was, he guessed, the one she'd been milking the first morning he'd come to the Wagler farm.

"This is Faith," Leanna said with a smile that seemed to encompass the *boppli*, the goat...and him. "Faith is the boss, and she never lets any of the others, including me, forget it. Once she's your friend, they all will love you, too."

He realized she was talking for his benefit because neither Heidi nor the goat could comprehend her words. She was trying to reassure him again the *bopplin* would be safe with her goats.

His heart softened as he watched Heidi touch the brown-and-white goat. The little girl snatched back her fingers before reaching out again. Her deep laugh swelled into the afternoon when she buried her fingers in Faith's coat. She leaned her cheek against the goat's head, then patted the goat's face, attention that he was surprised the animal accepted as her due.

"See?" Leanna asked without looking over her shoulder. "The *kinder* are safe with the goats and me."

"I should never have doubted that." He resisted stretching out as Harley patted the goat's haunch. When Leanna lifted him from the wagon so he could explore Faith as his sister was doing, Gabriel added, "You've always been cautious. You're someone who looks before you leap."

"Almost always." The words were so soft he wasn't sure if he'd heard her right.

Regret flooded him anew. She had to be referring to walking out with him. If only he could be honest with her...

Leanna stood and put the *bopplin* into the wagon. The goat wandered off to join the rest of the herd.

After closing the gate, she pulled the wagon around so the *kinder* could see him. They held up their arms, and he knelt and gave each a hug and a kiss on the head. The *bopplin* babbled with excitement, and he wondered if they were trying to tell him about the goats. Heidi was bouncing as she had on Leanna's lap while Harley leaned against the wagon's panel and grinned up at him.

"I'd say the visit to the goats was a success," Gabriel said, standing.

"They took to the herd as if they'd been around goats their whole lives." Leanna smiled. "Heidi astonishes me. She's curious about everything while Harley is content to observe his world. Was Freda like Harley?"

He flinched, unable to halt himself. Why was Leanna asking about Freda? Had he exposed the truth he wasn't the *bopplin*'s *daed* without realizing it?

As if he'd asked aloud, she said, "Maybe you don't want to talk about Freda. I understand that, because it's been such a short time since she died. However, I don't know anything about her because I never met her. I see how much Heidi resembles you, and I'm curious whom Harley takes after because they seem to have such different personalities."

"More like Freda's *daed*." He warned himself not to overreact to what was an obvious question. In fact, he was amazed Leanna hadn't asked about Freda sooner. "Freda was a lot like Heidi. I remember when she first started school. She wanted to poke her nose into every book there, even ones she wouldn't be using for years."

"*Ja*, that sounds like Heidi." Her smile fell away. "When you hugged Harley, did you notice his wheezing?"

"He seemed to be breathing harder, but I assumed it's because he's excited. Do you think he's allergic to your goats?"

"He drinks their *milch*, but they're dusty, so he might be allergic to dust."

"I never noticed that, and our house was thick with dust before you started keeping it clean."

"You may want to mention it to his *doktor* the next time you take him in."

"I'll try to remember."

"*Gut*. If—"

"Gabriel!" called Juanita as she jumped off the porch. Running to where they stood, she grinned. "You're coming to school on Friday, ain't so?"

He almost asked what Friday was, then wondered how he could have forgotten the eighth-grade graduation. Last week, he'd been counting down the days, the hours, the minutes until Juanita would be done with school so she could take Leanna's place watching the *bopplin.* He was startled. He hadn't done that during Leanna's second week at the farm.

He resisted the longing to ask her to stay on, because he guessed the people she cleaned houses for would be anxious for her to work for them. In addition, Juanita having a responsible job would satisfy the vocational study requirements the State of New York had set for plain scholars who didn't attend school until they were sixteen as *Englischers* did.

"I wouldn't miss it," he said.

"Gut!" Juanita clapped her hands as if she were as young as the twins. "We've been practicing our pieces for the past month. Not just the two of us graduating, but all the scholars. It's going to be a *wunderbaar* ceremony, and we want everyone in the hollow to attend."

"I'm sure most will." Leanna gave her sister a quick hug. "It is our first school graduation from our brand-new schoolhouse."

With a wave, Juanita rushed back into the house. The screen door slammed in her wake.

"You don't have to feel obligated to attend." Leanna stared at his boots.

"It will be a chance to see inside the school where the twins will be scholars in a few years."

"All right."

His fingers tilted her chin up before he could halt them. Astonishment bloomed in her eyes, and he hoped he hadn't made a horrific mistake. Since he'd touched her on the porch the night she'd given him the wagon, he hadn't been able to stop thinking about how much he longed for another chance to do so.

"Is everything really all right?" he asked.

"Everything is as it should be."

"You're avoiding answering my question."

"That's my answer." Her breath brushed his face as he leaned toward her.

"That everything is as it should be?"

"Ja."

"I wish I could believe you believe that, Leanna."

"You can."

Would she say the same thing if he asked if he could kiss her? He'd kissed her once. She'd been soft in his arms, her fingertips curved along his face as if she wanted to memorize it. Her lips had been welcoming, and his tingled at the memory.

"Gabriel!" she gasped.

"What?"

"You're smiling." She stared at him in disbelief.

"I guess I am." He felt his lips tip more.

She flung her arms around him as she whispered in his ear, "I've been praying you'd be happy again. *Danki* to God for opening your heart to joy again."

He was saved from having to answer when his brother came up the driveway and her sister called from the house at the same moment. As she hurried to help with whatever needed to be done inside, Michael stopped next to the wagon.

"Be careful, brother," he said without any other greeting. "Don't forget you broke her heart once already."

Gabriel tore his gaze from the porch and met his brother's eyes. "I can't ever forget that. Not ever."

Chapter Eight

The farmers market was held every Saturday morning during the summer in a small park at the center of the village of Salem. People still talked about the night the building that had stood there burned. It had held four shops and two apartments, and the fire began at 6:45 p.m. on a Tuesday. Because the fire siren was tested every Tuesday at 6:50 p.m., too few of the volunteer firefighters had realized there was an actual fire until the alarm was activated for a second time. By then, the fire had gained control of the old Victorian building, sending the residents fleeing with the clothes on their backs. The next morning a charred foundation and puddles filled with ashes were all that remained.

When it became obvious nobody was going to rebuild, the village took over the property. A gazebo was set in the center, and trees and flower beds planted. Narrow sidewalks crisscrossed the park. Many of the village *kinder* had learned to roller skate there, safe from vehicle traffic and pedestrians.

During the week, the benches were empty, but on Saturday mornings from May until September when the farmers market was held, no empty seats could be found.

Along with shoppers and those who'd come to talk and browse, *kinder* and dogs on leashes had gathered for a contest. They wore costumes, and Leanna wasn't sure who was fidgeting more: the *kinder* or the dogs, which came in a wide variety of shapes, sizes and colors. She guessed the dogs were supposed to be other types of animals. One was a black-and-white cow, because she could see a pink udder hanging down. Another one, a black pug, was showing off her rabbit ears and a tail made out of cotton balls.

Leanna couldn't wait for the market to close for the day. Each time she spoke with a stranger, it was a strain. She couldn't be like the other vendors who called out to neighbors, urging them to come and check out their wares. Instead, she sat behind the table she'd covered with a white cloth. Stacked on it were the bars of soap she'd made during the winter. A single hand-lettered sign listed what she had to sell and for how much. Since she didn't have an awning as many of the other sellers did, she'd been relieved to discover her spot was in the shade of the neighboring building.

A blonde stopped in front of the table. She looked close to Leanna's twenty-five years, but it wasn't always easy to tell with *Englischers* who wore makeup. Her close-cropped curls framed her round face, and she smiled as she asked, "Is this right? You made soap out of goats' milk?"

"That and other things like oatmeal and scents."

The woman picked up the bar and held it to her nose. "Oh, lavender. That's my favorite."

"I think it's a relaxing scent for enjoying a bath after a long day's work."

"Exactly." The woman grinned. "I'll take three bars."

Leanna told her the total price while putting the bars

into one of the paper bags she'd collected during the winter. Handing the bag to the woman, she made change.

"Are you here every week?" the woman asked.

"I hope to be, but it depends on how my goats cooperate."

The woman laughed. "I can see how that could be a problem." Her eyes widened as she glanced past Leanna. "Your family is here to help, I see."

Looking over her shoulder, Leanna's greeting to her siblings vanished when she saw Gabriel pulling the twins in the wagon she'd given him.

He surveyed the market booths with the same curiosity his daughter did.

"Good morning," he said to the blonde, then switched to *Deitsch*. "*Gute mariye*, Leanna."

The blonde grinned broadly before she walked to the next booth, but turned and winked.

Had it been aimed at her or Gabriel? Had he noticed as he bent to settle Harley in the wagon?

"What are you doing here?" she asked, horrified by how anxiety heightened her voice.

Gabriel chucked Harley under the chin before facing Leanna. He suspected she was doing well at the market. Only a few bars of soap remained on top of the table, and the pair of baskets by her black sneakers were empty. Her hands were clasped in her lap, making her look ill at ease while other sellers and customers bustled through the space between the small square and the road.

"I decided to see what all the talk about the farmers market is about," he said.

"And what do you think?"

He glanced around the score of tables and the people milling between them, stopping to talk with vendors and other shoppers. "I think," he said, realizing Leanna was waiting for him to answer, "I need to find the place where they're selling the fudge I see some kids eating."

"Third table to the left." She pointed.

"I'll make sure I don't miss it while we're walking around." He glanced at the wagon. "This design is truly clever."

"I thought they'd enjoy it."

"No question about that." He gave a wave and pulled the wagon up a cut in the curb.

As he wandered around the tables, talking with people he recognized and answering questions about the twins from people whom he hadn't met, he kept glancing at Leanna. He was pulled to her like a yo-yo, dancing on its string. No matter how interesting the articles were on the other tables, his thoughts returned to her.

He gave in to those thoughts and returned to her table. When Leanna asked how he'd liked the fudge, he realized he'd forgotten to sample any.

Rather than admit that, he asked, "Would you like some ice cream?"

When she smiled and nodded, he was glad she wasn't thinking about the last time he'd invited her to join him for ice cream. His heart lurched as he couldn't keep from wondering what she would have said that day if he'd asked her—as he'd planned—to become his wife.

"Are you planning to share with the *bopplin*?" she asked as she stood and began to fold the white tablecloth.

"A bite or two at least."

"Then we should get sorbet. It'll be less likely to bother their stomachs."

"I didn't think of that," he said before he could halt himself. He must sound like the world's worst *daed*.

She smiled. "It's hard to remember everything that contains cows' *milch*."

"Ice cream should be easy to remember."

The wrong words, because her smile wavered, and he knew she was thinking of how they had been going to meet in Strasburg on what should have been a special day for them.

"Maybe someone makes ice cream out of the *milch* from goats," he said, unable to bear the silence between them.

"Unlikely."

"You can't make ice cream from it?"

"You can, but it's thinner than regular ice cream. If you put it in the freezer, it becomes like a slab of granite." A smile flitted across her face. "I know, because I tried a few times until my family begged me to stop using them as guinea pigs for my experiments."

He was about to ask another question, but halted. The twins were getting antsy and ready to climb out of the wagon. At least Heidi was, and it seemed to Gabriel as if Harley was egging her on. He didn't dare to turn his back on the twins while helping Leanna pack up her empty baskets and put them in the Waglers' buggy, parked in front of the grocery store up the street. It took longer than he'd expected to walk the short distance because vendors kept stopping Leanna to ask if she'd be there next week.

"Your soap is such a hit!" exclaimed an *Englisch* woman whose black braid hung past her waist. "People stop there and then at my table to look at my jewelry. Maybe we should consider a cross-promotion."

"It's something to think about, Iris." With a wave, Leanna crossed Main Street during a break in the Saturday morning traffic.

"Do you think the bishop will be okay with you

doing promotion for your products?" Gabriel asked while she stored her supplies in the buggy.

"No, but Iris is a nice woman, and I didn't want to say no without checking."

"You're a nice woman, too, Leanna Wagler."

A blush rose up her cheeks, and she bowed her head to hide her face. He wanted to tell her such a motion was useless. After hours of re-creating her expressions while he stared at the ceiling, he could imagine how lovely the color looked against her black hair.

She checked to make sure her horse was all right. When she walked with him to the sidewalk, she began to talk about the farmers market as if it were the most important subject on the planet.

He listened as they strolled past the bank in a grand Victorian house and toward the hardware store, knowing this was her way of dealing with his compliment. Thinking back to when they'd been walking out together, he knew he must have praised her at least once.

Hadn't he?

He realized he had…though only in his mind. He hadn't wanted to embarrass her. It shocked him to discover that, before Aden asked him to save his daughter's reputation, Gabriel hadn't been honest with Leanna. He'd thought she was the loveliest, kindest, most fun girl he'd ever spent time with; yet he'd never hinted that to her.

No wonder she'd thought the worst of him when she learned he was marrying Freda. How could he fault Leanna for not responding to his earnest letter when he'd never told her how he felt about her?

He hadn't changed his mind about Leanna, and, as he listened to her lilting voice and saw her smile when she paused to speak with vendors packing up after the farmers market, he knew he must be careful. If he spoke the truth to her about anything, he might slip and reveal everything.

The twins crowed with delight as two large dogs walked past them. He slowed the wagon, after asking the dog owners' permission to pet the dogs.

"They're fascinated with dogs," Leanna said. "You should get them one."

He shook his head. "No."

"*Kinder* love dogs."

"I know."

Her smile vanished at his clipped tone. "What is it, Gabriel?"

"What do you mean?"

"I know that expression. You wear it when you're thinking about when you were young and everything in your life changed. Did you and Michael have a dog?"

"Ja." He should have guessed he couldn't hide from her keen eyes. He might as well tell her, so he could stave off her curiosity with more recent events. "We had a dog before we moved in with Aden. Red didn't get along with the Girods' dog, so he was given to another family. We never saw him again."

"I'm sorry. You must have been heartbroken."

"We were. It'd seemed, at the time, a sorrow as great as losing our parents." He took a deep breath and released it. "That's why I think the twins are better off without a dog."

"It's not a decision you have to make today."

Smiling in response to her kind words seemed the most natural response. When she stared at him, astonished, before she returned his smile, he knew why he hadn't given in to his yearning to smile before. The emotion arcing between them was invisible but as powerful as the sunlight burning through his straw hat.

His fingers tingled in a silent plea to reach them

out and take her hand. He tried to ignore them. Such a public display on the street busy with *Englischers* and a few plain folk would reflect poorly on Leanna. He couldn't risk that.

Gabriel stopped before they reached the intersection at the heart of the village. "Here we are."

The building was three stories high. The upper floors were painted pale gray. The dark red trim around the windows matched the color of the ground floor. Rolled red-and-white-striped awnings hung over the two sets of storefronts. Large windows flanked the doors. A third door between the stores led to the apartments on the top two floors.

The left-hand shop sold fabrics, and the other was their destination. Gold letters arched in the windows announced the shop sold candy and ice cream and other treats. Double screen doors at the top of three steps were open to catch the late-spring breezes and invite pass-ersby in to enjoy a snack.

When he pulled the wagon to one side of the steps where it wouldn't be in anyone's way, he wasn't sur-prised Leanna picked up Harley at the same time he reached for Heidi, who held her tiny arms up to him. He and Leanna had learned how to work in concert to take care of the twins. Would he develop the same easy rapport with Juanita as he had with Leanna?

Impossible!

Though in some ways it would be much simpler to have the teenager around his house. He almost snick-ered as he wondered if he were the first adult ever to have such a thought.

Juanita would do a *gut* job for him, and the drama that annoyed Michael would be gone. It was for the best.

It was!

If that was the truth, why couldn't he think of anything but how he'd miss the sound of Leanna's voice? He'd be sorry not to view the brightness of the *bopplin's* eyes when they saw her and the scent of her floral shampoo and the twinkle in her own eyes before she said something outrageous and… The list went on and on.

"All set?" Leanna asked.

Relieved to be freed from his thoughts, he settled Heidi against him so she could look past his shoulder and not miss anything. "All set."

Gabriel let Leanna precede him up the steps. Inside the shop, the wood floors might once have been polished or painted, but any hint of finish had been worn away. On one side, two great glass cases displayed wares the store would have sold when it first opened its doors. He glanced at boxes for candies that were no longer produced, and then his gaze was caught by the magnificent soda fountain.

A marble slab was set atop a carved bar more than ten feet long. Six cast-iron stools with bright red vinyl seats marched in front of it. Beyond the bar were the goose-necked dispensers for soda water and flavored drinks. The preparation area ran the full length of the bar, large folding doors on top of the freezer for the containers of ice cream. Smaller compartments must hold toppings and other supplies. Fluted dishes for sundaes were arranged before a huge mirror that reached to the ceiling. One corner of the mirror had a crack about as long as his hand, but the rest looked as pristine as the day it'd been put up, which he guessed must be close to a century before.

"This is amazing," he said in a whisper.

"Isn't it?" Leanna laughed. "You'd never guess this was in here if you drove past. Who'd imagine a little farm town would have such a fancy ice cream parlor?"

A cheerful man behind the counter gave them a big grin. "What can I do for you today?" He wiped the counter with a cloth though it looked clean. "Maybe an ice-cream soda? A banana split? An egg cream?"

"What's that?" Gabriel asked.

"It's soda water and cream and flavoring. I can make chocolate, vanilla or strawberry for you."

"No eggs?"

The man laughed. "Not a one. And don't ask me why they're called egg creams. Nobody seems to know, but they're good."

"It does sound *gut*, but we've got two lactose-intolerant twins here, so we need to skip anything with cream in it."

"We were thinking sorbet would be okay for them," Leanna added.

The man nodded. "It's your best bet." He pointed to a list over his right shoulder. "Those are the flavors we have."

Gabriel scanned the list. "I'll have raspberry. A medium. What about you, Leanna?"

"Strawberry. Small for me."

"A cone or a dish?" asked the man behind the counter.

"A dish for me." She smiled at the twins. "I think it'll make it easier to share."

"For me, too," Gabriel said.

The man grinned and went to fill the order. The servings were more generous than Gabriel had expected, so he was glad he hadn't ordered a large bowl. He paid for their treat, then led the way to a small metal table and pulled out two of the metal chairs. The metal backs had been twisted to match the heart shape of Leanna's *kapp*. Setting his dish on the white tabletop, he sat and settled Heidi on his lap. She quivered with excitement when she saw the colorful sorbet in front of him.

He gave her a little bit on a spoon, and her nose wrinkled. "Don't you like it?"

"Give her another bite." Leanna was offering a bit of her own to Harley. "That's not her 'I don't like it' face. It's her 'I don't know what it is because I've never had it before' face."

When he held up the spoon to Heidi again, she opened her mouth. She giggled when the sweet flavor rushed down her throat.

"You're right," he said.

"I've learned most of her expressions. Heidi doesn't hide anything about the way she feels. She wants the world to know. Harley is more circumspect, like you."

He took a bite of the sorbet to hide his reaction. It was simple with everyone else, even his brother, to hide the truth, but it was difficult not to share it with her. If only Aden hadn't asked him not to reveal the truth about his daughter...

"Da-da-da-da," Heidi said, patting his chest with each impatient repetition.

"Ja." Leanna smiled. "That's your *daed*. Aren't you going to answer her, Gabriel?"

"She's making nonsense sounds," he argued, holding out the spoon to Heidi again so he didn't have to look across the table. "She does that all the time."

"She does, but not that sound. She's talking to you, *daed*."

He readied a curt retort, but the sound wouldn't emerge past his lips as he stared at the *kind*. She believed he should understand what she was saying.

His throat filled with emotions, too many to examine a single one, as he wondered if she really was trying to say *"daed."* Once the *bopplin* began making sounds, he had been curious when one would come out with a real word. He never once allowed himself to imagine that word would be a *boppli*'s version of *daed*.

The enormity of the future swarmed over him. Heidi and Harley would grow up calling him that. At some time, he needed to be honest with them. When and how? Would they see his letting them think he was their *daed* as a deception or would they accept the truth and go on with their lives?

A bit of ironic laughter surged in his clogged throat. How would their lives change when he spoke the truth? He couldn't keep it from them forever.

Soft fingers settled on his hand fisted around the spoon. Raising his gaze from her hand to Leanna's compassionate eyes, he heard her speak a single word.

"Don't."

"Don't what?"

"Don't go wherever you went with your thoughts," she said. "Whether it was the past or the future, don't go there. *This* is a happy moment. Stay here with us."

"There's nothing else I'd rather do."

His sincere words brought a scintillating smile from her. *"Gut,"* she said before offering Harley another bite of her sorbet.

She was right. He was going to enjoy this special time with her and the twins because he wasn't sure if there ever should be another.

As he listened to Leanna teasing both *kinder*, he knew there were a lot of things about his future he needed to consider. He must be careful before he hurt the people he cared about.

Again.

Chapter Nine

Leanna looked up at the clock on the kitchen wall. It was only ten, but she felt as if she'd put in a day's work. Nothing had gone right. She'd overslept and had to rush getting dressed. Somehow, she'd failed to put all the pins in her hair and her *kapp*, so now she had to keep pushing both into place each time she moved.

When she'd arrived at the Millers' farm, Gabriel had been curt. Not just to her, but to his twin and his *kinder*. Michael had given her a quick shrug before he followed Gabriel out the door, showing he didn't know what was bothering his twin.

The *bopplin* acted as out of sorts as their *daed*. Harley spit out every bite of oatmeal she tried to feed him. Heidi refused to eat or play with her toys. The little girl kept rubbing her eyes and yawning as she alternated between crying and whining, and Leanna wondered if the whole family was exhausted by everything that had happened since they'd left Lancaster County.

A knock came at the door, and Leanna considered ignoring it. The kitchen was a mess, the *bopplin* were covered with bits of food, and she must look a sight with her *kapp* threatening to fall over her right ear. Taking a deep breath, she opened the door.

"Miriam!" She hadn't expected to see her friend at the Millers' house.

"You look as if you're having a dandy of a day." The tall blonde walked in and surveyed the kitchen. Without saying anything further to Leanna, she picked up Heidi and asked, "What's bothering you so much you have to tell the whole world about it?"

The *boppli* regarded Miriam with curiosity. Sticking her thumb in her mouth, Heidi became silent.

"You should have come earlier and convinced her to be quiet." Leanna lifted Harley out of his chair. "Do you have time to stay and visit for a while? Once I get him cleaned, I can put on the teapot."

When Leanna faced her friend, Miriam gave her the stern look she usually aimed at a recalcitrant scholar. "You can't have forgotten!"

"I could, because it seems I have." She resisted a yawn of her own. Too many dreams of Gabriel opening his arms to her—last night's had been in a new location: in front of the ice-cream shop—had jolted her awake in the middle of the night. After almost too many nights of various versions of the sweet fantasy, she had no idea if her dream-self had ever accepted his invitation to hug or not. It was as if her mind didn't trust her with that information because it feared she would give in to her yearnings to be near him when she was awake.

She'd never expected her brain to have to protect her from her heart. It was unsettling to think about.

"Didn't Juanita and Kenny remind you this morning?" Miriam's question saved her from her disconcerting thoughts.

"They may have, but I arrived here this morning in

time to discover the *bopplin* were refusing to take their bottles. And then the morning got more frantic after that." Even in her own ears, the excuse sounded weak, but how could she speak of her tumultuous thoughts to her *gut* friend Miriam?

"Today is the school picnic down by the creek." Miriam grinned at Heidi, who gave her a shy smile in return. "I know *you* want to go and have fun with the other *kinder*. How about you, Leanna?"

"Of course I want to go." She rolled her eyes. "I can't believe I forgot the school picnic. Juanita and Kenny have been talking about it nonstop."

"You've had a few other things on your mind."

"*Ja*, these two."

"And their *daed*? Annie told me yesterday at the bakery that you and Gabriel walked out together before he married the *bopplin's mamm*."

"We did." She took Harley to the sink to wash thick blotches of oatmeal off before it hardened on his clothes. With her back to her friend, she added, "It didn't work out as either of us hoped when we first met."

"I'm sorry. Is it uncomfortable for you taking care of his *kinder*?"

"It was at first. It's not now." Leanna was amazed to realize that was the truth. She never would have imagined she could become accustomed to the crazy situation in which she and Gabriel had found themselves. Yet when they'd taken the *bopplin* for sorbet on Saturday, it had seemed natural to be with him and his family.

"I'm glad to hear that."

"Me, too." And that was almost the truth. She wondered if it was possible ever to fall out of love with someone. The hopes she'd savored during those few months had left a permanent shadow on a corner of her

Get Up To 4 Free Books!

Dear Reader,

IT'S A FACT: if you answer 4 quick questions, we'll send you 4 FREE REWARDS from each series you try!

Try **Love Inspired® Romance Larger-Print** books featuring Christian characters facing modern-day challenges.

Try **Love Inspired® Suspense Larger-Print** novels featuring Christian characters facing challenges to their faith... and lives

Or **TRY BOTH!**

I'm not kidding you. As a leading publisher of women's fiction, we value your opinions... and your time. That's why we are prepared to reward you handsomely for completing our mini-survey. In fact, we have 4 Free Rewards for you, including 2 free books and 2 free gifts from each series you try!

Thank you for participating in our survey,

Pam Powers

To get your 4 FREE REWARDS:
Complete the survey below and return the insert today to receive up to 4 FREE BOOKS and FREE GIFTS guaranteed!

"4 for 4" MINI-SURVEY

1 Is reading one of your favorite hobbies?
☐ YES ☐ NO

2 Do you prefer to read instead of watch TV?
☐ YES ☐ NO

3 Do you read newspapers and magazines?
☐ YES ☐ NO

4 Do you enjoy trying new book series with FREE BOOKS?
☐ YES ☐ NO

Please send me my Free Rewards, consisting of **2 Free Books from each series I select** and **Free Mystery Gifts**. I understand that I am under no obligation to buy anything, as explained on the back of this card.

❏ **Love Inspired® Romance Larger-Print** (122/322 IDL GNPV)
❏ **Love Inspired® Suspense Larger-Print** (107/307 IDL GNPV)
❏ **Try Both** (122/322/107/307 IDL GNP7)

FIRST NAME   LAST NAME

ADDRESS

APT.#   CITY

STATE/PROV.   ZIP/POSTAL CODE

READER SERVICE—Here's how it works:

heart, something she'd decided should be filed under "older but wiser" experiences.

Not wanting to think about that, she left Miriam playing with the twins. Leanna concentrated on collecting extra clothing, food and bottles for the *bopplin*, as well as some of their favorite toys. She put two small quilts in the wagon, then added a pair of towels because the picnic would be beside the water and the *kinder* loved splashing in their baths. Because she knew Gabriel would be concerned if he came home and they weren't there, she left a note on the kitchen table explaining where they were.

As she pulled the twins' wagon behind her, Leanna was relieved Miriam spent the five minutes it took for them to walk along the road talking about her scholars. Though Miriam was looking forward to the opportunity to spend time at home with her husband, Eli, and his nephew, Kyle, she admitted she'd miss teaching. She'd stayed on an extra year and had been training the blacksmith's sister, Grace Streicher, to take her place. The girl had moved from Canada to manage her brother James's house a month ago, and she'd agreed to help at the school when it became obvious there was nobody else who could.

Leanna pulled the wagon down the narrow path from the road. Stones and tree roots jutted out of the ground at odd angles, threatening to tip it. She edged to the side to let four scholars surge past her. Knowing they had their sights set on the creek at the bottom of the hill, she doubted if they'd noticed her much slower passage along the rough path.

She heard the waterfall before she saw it. Only about five feet high, the cascade sent water into a deep pool in the otherwise shallow creek. No wonder the *kinder* had claimed the area for a swimming hole.

The open glade along the creek's bank was beautiful. Trees surrounded it and lined the far side of the creek, but no underbrush crowded the shore. Gravel edged the pool, offering a place for the younger *kinder* to play beside the water. Someone had mowed the grass enough for the *mamms* to spread out blankets. Sitting there, they could keep a close eye on the pool and the waterfall dropping into it.

Leanna smiled when she saw the other two members of the Harmony Creek Spinsters Club, her sister and Sarah, sitting in the shadow of some ancient trees that stretched their branches over the creek. The leaves filtered the sunshine, setting it to dance on the water flying over boulders farther down the creek.

Sarah had hair as red as Gabriel's and wore new glasses. When Sarah explained she'd taken a tumble off a horse and broken her old ones, Leanna was glad that was the only damage her friend had suffered. Sarah always told amusing stories, something she'd learned in order to entertain four *Englisch kinder* when she was their nanny. She soon had everyone sitting around her laughing about how a beaver had helped itself to some of the trees her brothers had chopped down and planned to cut in their sawmill.

"For some reason, nobody wants wood that's already been gnawed," Sarah finished. "Menno was annoyed, but Benjamin reminded him the beavers were getting revenge for the two of them breaking up a new dam on the farm pond. The dam had blocked the flow of water, and my brothers need it to get big logs from the woodlot to their sawmill. Also, far more important to Benjamin is that the dam meant losing *gut* fishing."

"Has Menno calmed down?" asked Leanna, knowing Sarah's two brothers had once tried to run her life. That had changed, but her elder brother Menno had little patience with anyone or anything else.

"I have faith he will…eventually."

That brought more laughter as the rest of the scholars and their *mamms* and younger siblings joined them beside the creek. Everyone pulled out food to share, and the conversation was interlaced with recipes, as well as for calls for the *kinder* to be careful in the water.

As she chatted with her friends, Leanna was kept busy chasing Heidi to keep her from the water. After they'd finished picking up from their picnic, she decided to take the *bopplin* to enjoy the water.

"Before you go…" Miriam said as Leanna threw the towels over her shoulder and bent to pick up the twins. "I have some news, but you can't share it with anyone. Not your husbands, not your families."

"What is it?" Annie's eyes twinkled. "Is it what I think it is?"

"Promise first. No telling anyone."

After all three vowed they'd keep Miriam's secret, she put her hands around her abdomen. "The secret's right here."

"You're going to have a *boppli*!" Leanna exclaimed as the others grinned. "When?"

"In November. Around Thanksgiving time." Her voice was flush with joy.."My timing was off. I wish I'd been done teaching school before I had to deal with morning sickness."

Sarah laughed. "We're going to have to change the name of our group to the Harmony Creek Spinsters, Newlyweds and New *Mamms* Club. Who would have guessed our lives would change so much in a year?"

Leanna forced a smile when the rest joined in with Sarah's laughter. It was true their lives had changed. She wished she knew what her life was changing into. Gabriel was in it, but not in any way she would have imagined when she'd first heard of his wedding plans. She'd always been sure of what she wanted. A *wunderbaar* romance with an exciting man like in the books she used to read.

Odd... She couldn't remember the last time she'd picked up a novel and let herself be drawn into the story of two people falling in love. Was that because she wasn't sure if such a tale would ever come true for her?

Gabriel wiped sweat off his nape as he edged down the already well-worn path toward the creek. The sound of happy voices drifted through the thick leaves, but he couldn't see the water or any of the people gathered there. Stepping around a blackberry bush, being careful to avoid its thorns, he saw a clearing below. The only thing in it was the red wagon Leanna had given the twins.

He'd been surprised when he got home after finishing a hard morning's work on the studio in West Rupert to find a note from Leanna on the kitchen table. She hadn't said anything to him before about taking the twins on a picnic. It wasn't like her to be so secretive.

"No," his brother had said, "that's what you are, Gabriel."

Michael's words continued to ring in his ears, another reminder of how much he hated being restrained by the promise he'd made. Gabriel had considered going to Eli Troyer, their minister, to seek his advice but hadn't. How could he explain to Eli how he no longer believed God heard his prayers?

Those thoughts vanished when he rounded a corner on the path and caught sight of Leanna squatting by a pool. The sunlight glistened with blue fire on her black hair and added warmth to her cheeks, which were a shade lighter than the dark rose dress puddling around her bare feet. Beside her, Harley sat close enough to slap his hands in the pool. Each time his palms hit the water, he chortled with delight. Leanna was holding Heidi up so she could stamp her tiny feet, sending drops in every direction. When a few hit her brother, Harley shook his head and just kept playing in the pool, too.

It was an enticing sight, a view of a woman spending time with two *kinder* she loved. He paid no attention to the older *kinder* lining up to slide with the quick current down the waterfall and into the pool. A group of women sitting on blankets beneath the trees to his right barely registered in his mind.

Walking as if drawn by an invisible cord toward Leanna and the twins, he paused behind her. She looked up, and their gazes fused. He couldn't pull his eyes away. Not that he wanted to, because he could have stayed there forever. It was a moment out of time, as it had been the night he first saw her.

"Hi," she said.

"Hi." Not great conversation, but the single word seemed perfect.

The moment was shattered when Heidi let out an impatient cry. Leanna shifted the little girl so she could splash in the water more.

Gabriel took a steadying breath, feeling as if he was waking from the best dream he'd ever had. His contentment vanished when he noticed how blue the twins' lips looked.

"They need to get out of the water," he said.

"Why?"

"Look at them! They're blue with the cold!"

Leanna laughed. "They're blue from the ice pops they had a few minutes ago." She turned Heidi so he could see drops of the same color down the front of the little girl's once-pristine *schlupp schotzli*. "I think they got more on them than in their mouths. I figured I could wash them and let them play at the same time."

More than a bit embarrassed, Gabriel said, "Let me help."

"*Danki*. Can you say hi to your *daed*?" She wiggled Heidi's hand in a greeting as she handed him a towel. "Your *daed* wants to get you cleaned up."

"Da-da-da," Heidi chanted, curling up her toes in delight.

He glanced at Harley, but the little boy seemed interested only in how much of his tiny fist he could cram into his mouth.

"Don't worry," Leanna said. "He'll talk in his own time. I've been told I didn't talk to anyone but Annie until I was almost three. I let Annie talk for us, and it looks as if Harley is doing the same with Heidi. When I did start talking to everyone, *Grossmammi* Inez said I spoke in full sentences. She said it probably was the first time I could get a word in edgewise. Don't worry about Harley. He'll talk when he's ready."

"You're right." He dipped one corner of the towel into the water. Dabbing at Harley's face, he chuckled when the little boy screwed up his mouth to thwart him.

"You're laughing." Astonishment heightened Leanna's voice.

"I've been known to from time to time."

"Not since you've moved here."

He finished washing Harley and looked at her. "I'm sure I have—"

"Not once. You've smiled." A flush rose up her face.

"I'm sorry, Gabriel. I shouldn't be teasing you when it's been such a short time since…"

He didn't need her to finish. He knew what she'd been about to say. *Since your wife died.*

She frowned at Harley. "Let me clean him up."

"I did."

"You did? His lips are still blue."

Gabriel looked at the *boppli* and saw she was right. "The water is chilly."

"He didn't go into the water. I've kept a close watch on them, so they didn't get too cold."

"He's been laughing a lot?"

"Ja."

"Well, there you go. You know he can laugh so hard he ends up coughing. It makes him short of breath. He's always fine in a few minutes."

"Always?"

"Leanna, it's been less than a month since you first met them. I've known them their whole lives. Don't you think I'm more familiar with what's going on with them?"

"Sometimes fresh eyes see things others haven't noticed."

"He's fine. Look at him." He motioned toward the *kinder.*

She started to retort, but must have thought better of it. She stood and settled Heidi on her hip before she began to pick up the *bopplin*'s toys and put them into the wagon.

"Do you want some help?" he asked.

"No, I'm fine."

He resisted the yearning to tell her he agreed. It might push her further away.

"I shouldn't have said that, Leanna."

"Said what?"

She wasn't going to make this easy for him. And why should she? He had been the one to ruin the fun they were having with the *kinder*.

"The truth is," he replied, "your question poked at a sore spot."

"Your worry that you aren't a *gut daed*?"

"How—?"

She smiled at him with as much compassion as she did the twins. "You may think you're keeping it a secret, but it colors everything you do, Gabriel. These *bopplin* are such a part of you, and you want to give them all you can so they have a *wunderbaar* childhood. Shall I tell you something else that isn't a secret?"

"Ja." If she had discovered the truth about the pledge he'd made to Aden, then it'd be better for him to find out. How had she learned about what nobody else living knew?

She crooked her finger and motioned for him to lean closer. When he did, she said, "It's no secret you're succeeding much better than you seem to think you are."

Leanna couldn't keep from smiling when she saw the amazement and then relief in Gabriel's eyes. Was he so worried about being a *daed*? He must be, and she must make sure she pointed out—in a casual manner that would not lead him to suspect she was trying to bolster his confidence—what he was doing well for his *kinder*.

Putting the *bopplin* into the wagon gave her the excuse to move away from him before she did something crazy like running her fingers along his cheek or pressing her lips to it. She must have lost her mind to be thinking of doing such things when her twin and their friends were sitting ten feet away.

Gabriel reached for the wagon's handle at the same time she did. His fingers closed over hers, and he arched his brows. Was he daring her to tug her hand away from his? *Ja*, he was!

Joy surged through her. This afternoon, he had become, for a few minutes, the man she'd walked out with, a man who chuckled and enjoyed teasing her. She'd begun to believe that man was gone and would never return. Hope filled her, something that hadn't happened in so long she couldn't remember the last time she'd enjoyed the sensation.

"Do you think it'll take two of us to pull the wagon up to the road?" he asked, his smile returning.

"We wouldn't want it to slide backward and careen down the hill and into the water."

"It might be the only way to get their clothing clean." He glanced at the twins, and love for his *kinder* blossomed in his eyes.

How could he think he wasn't a *wunderbaar daed*? She must make an effort to confirm that for him in the few days she had left before Juanita came to the farm to take her place.

Chapter Ten

Gabriel finished shaving and reached for a towel to wipe bits of suds out of his beard. He grimaced at his reflection in the downstairs bathroom. It was vanity to be annoyed that his beard looked uneven. Curling and red, the fine hair refused to fill in.

"You look fine," teased Michael from beyond the open door. "It's not as if it's your *kinder* graduating today."

"I don't think I'm ready for teenagers yet." He tossed the towel onto the side of the sink and put away his shaving cup and razor. Pulling his suspenders up over his shoulders and into place, he added, "I don't know if I'll ever be."

"You'd better figure it out over the next twelve years because you'll be facing every growing-up phase times two."

"*Danki* for the reminder." He glanced into the mirror to make sure his collar was straight. "As if I needed it."

After going into the kitchen, he picked up his straw hat. He put it on his head before reaching down for the twins. Remembering how Leanna had taught him to pick up one, then the other, so he could carry both, he smiled at the *bopplin*.

"Let me help," Michael said.

"Danki." Gabriel motioned for his brother to take Heidi. His twin might tease him—a lot—but Gabriel was always able to depend on him to be there to help and to give his honest opinion. Honest? Gabriel wished he could be the same. *If only Aden hadn't asked him to promise not to reveal the truth that would hurt his daughter in the eyes of the community...* The words had been repeating endlessly through his head for the past few days.

Again he longed to reach out to God for guidance. At first, his anger at his Heavenly Father had been a scaffold, holding him up during the trying days and weeks in the wake of Freda's and Aden's deaths. How could Gabriel have guessed at the time he'd been using that support to build a wall between him and God?

"Don't take this the wrong way, Gabriel," his brother said as they walked out to their buggy, "but I hope you're prepared for today."

"It's not my graduation ceremony. I don't have to worry about reciting today."

Michael didn't smile at Gabriel's jest. "We've been walking on eggshells whenever Leanna's in the house. You're making such an effort to pretend you don't share a past you might as well be wearing signs that say 'Look at me. I'm over you.'" He scowled. "Of course, that would be a lie."

"Half a one maybe."

"You think you're over her?" Michael made a rude sound deep in his throat. "I still don't understand why you married Freda when you were in love with Leanna, but I've gotten tired of asking and getting the runaround. I've got *gut* eyes, and I can see you're not over her."

"I didn't say that. I think she's…" He didn't want to say the words out loud. They'd be too final, too forever.

He knew if Leanna walked out the door tomorrow and treated him with the coolness she'd shown when he'd first gone to the Waglers' farm to get goat *milch*, it would be better for them. He'd be able to keep the promises he'd made to Freda and to her *daed*, and Leanna could…

He was shocked he didn't know what Leanna wanted for the rest of her life. Marriage, he assumed. A woman who was as *gut* with *bopplin* as Leanna was should have her own. Yet, he hadn't seen any bachelors in the community paying her special attention. Were they out of their minds? Maybe Leanna wasn't a great cook, but the only way to a man's heart wasn't through his stomach.

Then his own stomach cramped. Maybe she was walking out with someone. He didn't know their neighbors well enough for them to pass along gossip from the Amish grapevine. The other unmarried men might not have taken notice of pretty Leanna because they knew one among them was courting her.

He couldn't inquire himself or get Michael to ask. His brother would refuse to become involved. He'd made it clear he didn't want to be part of what he called "the drama" any longer. To speak of Leanna to the other men in the settlement would be an announcement he was interested in her. He wasn't going to risk hurting her as he had before, and until he knew what he wanted for his family, how could he even consider making her a part of it?

He'd make a greater mess of her life than he had with Freda's. Hadn't Paul written in his letter to the Ephesians that a man should love and sacrifice for his wife as Christ loved and sacrificed Himself for the members of His church?

And Gabriel had failed to do that.

* * *

Everyone in the small plain community had gathered for the first graduation ceremony at the school that sat not far from the banks of Harmony Creek. The air of expectation sent the scholars racing from one group of adults to the next, so excited they couldn't stand still.

Leanna slowed the family's crowded buggy as she reached the small white building that was the community's school. She held her elbows close so she didn't bump her *grossmammi*. Usually there weren't more than two or three of them in the buggy at once. However, today Juanita had insisted she needed to ride because she didn't want to get dusty walking the half mile to school. Kenny had decided he shouldn't walk, either, though he wouldn't explain why.

So she and *Grossmammi* Inez sat in the front seat while Juanita and Kenny were cramped with Annie in the back. She was glad Miriam had decided to hold the graduation picnic earlier in the week instead of after the ceremony. Otherwise, there would be casseroles and desserts piled in the buggy with them.

"Hold on tight," she said as she turned the buggy off the road and onto the uneven ground where the scholars played ball.

Hearing groans from the rear, as well as laughter, she turned the horse toward where other buggies were parked. She gauged the distance to the school. It was farther than she'd hoped. Glancing at her *grossmammi*, she faltered. To say she was worried about *Grossmammi* Inez walking would embarrass the older woman.

"Waglers?" came a jovial shout.

Looking out the buggy, she saw Eli Troyer striding toward them. The man, who'd been ordained as the settlement's first minister earlier in the year, was married to Miriam.

"We saved a spot up front for you," Eli said when he came to stand beside the buggy.

"Danki." She made sure she was facing Eli when she spoke, so he could read her lips.

He'd become so adept at it that it was possible to forget he'd suffered a hearing loss in the tragic accident that had killed his sister and brother-in-law. He had to concentrate on what people were saying, but, as he'd joked more than once, it behooved a minister to pay close attention to what was being discussed.

"I don't need special consideration," grumbled her *grossmammi.*

"Of course not," Eli replied, "but we wanted to make sure our graduates' families had the best seats today. We'll never have another first graduation, so we want to celebrate it." With a wave, he motioned for Leanna to drive to the spot he'd pointed out.

"This sounds," *Grossmammi* Inez continued to complain, "like an excuse he and Miriam devised to make sure I got to the graduation on time."

"And we should always be grateful to those who treat us with unexpected kindness," Leanna said as she maneuvered the horse and buggy through the crowd. "I'm sure I've heard someone say that more than once."

"Me, too," said three voices from behind her.

The older woman chuckled and shook her head. "I should have known my own words would come back to taunt me one day."

"Gut advice is…" She bit her lip as a little boy almost stepped in front of the horse before his *daed* grabbed him and pulled him out of the way.

"Always *gut*, even if you don't want to listen to it," her *grossmammi* finished with another laugh.

"I've heard that from someone wise, too."

"Me, too!" crowed her siblings in unison from the back seat.

Everyone was laughing as Leanna stopped the buggy in the spot that Miriam pointed toward with a big smile.

As they piled out of the buggy, Juanita scanned the crowd. A pucker formed between her eyebrows.

"Isn't Gabriel coming?" she asked.

"He said he was, and he keeps his word." *Usually*, Leanna couldn't help adding. She shoved the thought aside.

She needed to heed the advice she'd given Gabriel. Juanita's graduation was a special moment, and thinking about anything else could mar it.

Offering her arm to her *grossmammi*, Juanita led the family into the schoolhouse. The desks had been pushed aside, and the benches they used for church had been arranged in the center of the room.

Leanna smiled as her younger sister almost ran to join the scholars by the teacher's desk at the front. The older *kinder* took their places behind the little ones, and Leanna wondered how long Miriam and her assistant, Grace, had practiced with her scholars. It was an important day for her friend as well, because this was Miriam's graduation, too. Leanna guessed her friend couldn't wait to become a full-time wife to their minister.

Sitting near the end of bench next to *Grossmammi* Inez and Annie, Leanna scanned the room. Where *was* Gabriel? She didn't see him or Michael or the *bopplin*.

Miriam walked to her desk and turned to the scholars, who looked at her eagerly. Grace, a petite blonde, stood on the other side of the scholars, ready to help when needed. Giving them a smile, Miriam shifted to face the parents and families who'd gathered in the schoolhouse. It would be celebrating the first anniversary of its opening in July because last year there had been an extra session to make up for days lost during the time the families were moving into the new settlement.

"*Danki* for coming today for Harmony Creek Hollow's first ever graduation ceremony," she said with a hint of pride no one would begrudge her today. "Our scholars have worked hard this year, and each one will be taking on new challenges in their new grades next year…except for our two graduates." She aimed a smile at Juanita and at Eugene Yoder, the other graduate. "Juanita and Eugene will be facing challenges of their own, which I know they're eager to begin. I doubt they'll miss their deskwork, but I suspect they'll recall fondly the softball games we've had this spring."

Indulgent laughter rippled through the room, and Leanna knew she wasn't the only one remembering the fun of being a scholar.

Miriam began the ceremony by asking her husband to say a prayer. Eli stood and spoke with his simple eloquence of how they needed God's guidance at beginnings as well as endings. When he said, "Amen," the scholars squared their shoulders as a group and began a hymn Leanna had also sung in school.

Leanna resisted looking around the room for Gabriel again. As they were in the second row, almost everyone would notice if she swiveled her head. Her nails cut into her palms, her fingers curled in frustration. She couldn't believe he wasn't going to keep his promise to Juanita. The only other reason he wouldn't be here was if something had gone wrong.

Dear God, don't let something have happened to the bopplin.

A hand on her shoulder brought her head up. Gabriel sat beside her, holding Heidi. The little girl raised her arms to Leanna, who took her before the *kind* could protest, interrupting the program.

Leaning toward her, Gabriel whispered, "I'm sorry we're late. Our horse threw a shoe, and we had to get him back to the farm."

"Is he okay?"

"He's fine, but Michael and I ended up pushing and pulling the buggy ourselves to the house."

Leanna put a hand over her mouth to keep from laughing. The sound wouldn't be welcome when the seven-year-olds were reciting the poems they'd written.

"How did you keep the twins from helping you?" she asked.

"Later," he whispered. "I'll give you the sad details."

Turning her attention to the scholars let Leanna hide how much she looked forward to their conversation after the graduation ceremony. She rocked Heidi on her lap, keeping the *boppli* entertained, though Heidi seemed fascinated with the scholars. When they sang, the little girl did her best to join in with them despite being seemingly fixated on a single note.

As soon as the ceremony was over, Miriam invited the guests to join her, the scholars and Grace outside for refreshments. The *kinder* rushed out the door, and Leanna guessed there would be one additional softball game for the two graduates to join.

Most of the men went to play with the youngsters, a special treat when crops and haying kept the *daeds* busy until dark six days a week. Michael, carrying Harley, stood on the sidelines as teams were chosen.

Gabriel was waiting by the steps as Leanna emerged from the school with Heidi. When she walked toward him, he was smiling. She wondered if she'd ever get accustomed to the *wunderbaar* sight after so many days of nothing but frowns?

"I imagine," she said with a feigned somber tone, "you're going to have sore muscles tomorrow after your workout today."

His smile broadened. "I'm glad everyone was already here, so nobody saw the dance Michael and I had to do as we pulled and pushed and checked to make sure the *bopplin* weren't trying to escape."

"It's *gut* you have those car seats in your buggy to keep them in place."

"Heidi has already managed to figure out how to loosen at least one strap. It won't take her long, knowing her as I do, for her to learn how to release them all. And Harley somehow got half his clothes off, though he was strapped in. I don't know how he manages it."

"He starts undressing whenever he's bored."

"You could have warned me."

She laughed. "Haven't you noticed how many times when you're coming in at night that I'm getting him dressed?"

"I thought he'd made a mess or something."

"No. He likes to take off his clothes and throw them at his sister. She thinks it's hilarious."

Before Gabriel could reply, Juanita raced up and flung her arms around him.

"You came! *Danki!*"

Again Leanna had to suppress her reaction. Not laughter this time, though Gabriel's expression of shock at her sister's exuberance was comical. A longing ached deep within her because she wanted to experience standing as close to him as her sister was. Would his warmth welcome her to lean against his sturdy chest?

She lowered her eyes before anyone could read her thoughts. *God*, she prayed, *You know Your plan for me. I know it's impatience that makes me ask You to reveal a bit of it to me, but I'm floundering. Please send me some guidance so I can live the life You want for me.*

"Leanna!" A shout came from across the schoolyard.

Michael ran toward her. People opened a path for him as they stared in dismay at the horror on his face.

Leanna understood why when Michael skidded to a stop in front of her and held out Harley, who was an odd shade of gray.

"He's choking on something!" Michael cried.

She shook her head. "I think he's having trouble catching his breath." Shoving Heidi into Gabriel's arms, she took the other *boppli*. She sat on the ground and put him on her bent knee. She rubbed his back in slow, gentle circles. "What were you doing before he started gasping?"

"We were playing a game of tickle."

"Was he laughing?"

"Ja." Michael exchanged a glance with his brother, and this time Leanna guessed what the silent look meant. He was apologizing for whatever was happening to his nephew. "He was having fun and laughing pretty hard."

Beneath her fingers, Harley shuddered as he drew in one breath, released it and then pulled in a second, deeper breath. The color in his face began to return to normal. Lifting him to her shoulder, she continued to caress his back as she stood.

"He's okay." She spoke so everyone listening could be reassured, though her words were for the Millers.

"He gets so excited when he laughs that he forgets

to breathe," Gabriel said as he put Heidi on the grass by his feet and took her twin. "I've seen it happen a few times before, and he's always fine afterward."

"You could have warned me." Michael released a sigh that countermanded his sharp words.

Gabriel shifted the *boppli* so he could see his son's now smiling face. "You didn't want anyone to forget you were here, ain't so?"

Leanna bit her lower lip. There must be more to Harley's breathing problem than what Gabriel seemed to believe, but now wasn't the time to question his assumptions.

Juanita ran over to them, smiling. "*Komm* and watch the rest of the game. You don't want to miss any of our celebration."

"Sounds fun," Michael said with a grin. "And in August, you'll have to come to the celebration at our house."

"What will you be celebrating?" Leanna asked.

"Birthdays."

"Weren't you and Gabriel born in January?"

"*Ja*, but the twins were born at the end of August."

"The twins will be a year old in August?" The words came out in a squeak as she turned to where Gabriel was grabbing for a quick-moving Heidi.

He froze and looked over his shoulder at her. His face was as ashen as Harley's had been minutes ago. Dismay and a stronger emotion filled his dark eyes. Fear?

Behind her, she heard a sharp gulp. Michael began to speak, but Gabriel waved him to silence. Michael frowned and stamped away. Juanita glanced at them, then spun to run back to the game.

Leanna started to ask Gabriel to explain, but halted when she saw Heidi had somehow made it to the top of the steps on the school's porch. Jumping forward,

Leanna grabbed the *boppli* before she could attempt to crawl down. She held the little girl close like a cloak to ward off the cold. The chill was inside her, oozing out of the most wounded parts of her heart.

"Danki," Gabriel said in an emotionless voice. "One of these days, she's going to fall on her nose, and maybe then she won't be so ready to explore." His attempt at humor was futile.

She walked to him. Though she was unsure she could speak louder than a whisper, she didn't want to chance anyone overhearing them.

"Is it true?" she asked. "Is their birthday in August?"

"Ja, at the end of the month," he said. "They will be nine months old next week."

"I thought they were younger."

"Lots of people do because they're small for their ages."

"So they'll really be a year old in August?" It was a stupid question, but she still couldn't wrap her mind around what he'd said.

"Ja," he repeated, and this time didn't add anything more.

After he gathered up both twins, he walked toward his buggy. He didn't slow. Would he stop if she called after him?

So many thoughts collided in her mind. The memory of *Grossmammi* Inez saying how twins were born early. The questions she had about how advanced Heidi seemed for her age.

No matter how she tried to rearrange the facts, they added up to one conclusion. Freda had been pregnant when Gabriel married her less than two weeks after the day he and Leanna were supposed to meet in Strasburg.

Chapter Eleven

After a sleepless night spent debating whether she should return to the Millers' farm or not when she could simply send Juanita and let her take over watching the *bopplin*, Leanna went through the motions of helping prepare breakfast for her family. Nobody complained about overcooked eggs and barely browned toast. Instead, they gave her sympathetic glances. She was grateful no one asked how she was feeling.

She had no idea.

She was strangled by hurt, puzzlement and disbelief. All the things she'd felt when she heard he was marrying Freda after he'd stood up Leanna and sent a letter she hadn't bothered to read. She hadn't cared what excuses he'd given her to explain why he was becoming someone else's husband without telling Leanna the truth face-to-face.

She should have been suffused with a sense of relief that she hadn't been wrong about how the twins didn't act the age Gabriel let her assume they were, but she wasn't. What was being right worth when she had to endure the pain as if for the first time?

Betrayed.

If someone had asked her how she felt, that would have been her answer. She couldn't say Gabriel had betrayed her…again. No, this time her heart had been the traitor. It had persuaded her to trust him while she welcomed his *kinder* into her heart, believing she was helping it heal.

How wrong she'd been!

She was sure her family noticed how little she said, but nobody, not even her older brother, Lyndon, who'd joined them for breakfast after finishing the milking with Kenny, mentioned it. That warned her that her silence wasn't fooling them. Usually Lyndon loved to tease her and his other siblings, but today he ate his food, talked about the weather and stood as soon as he'd cleaned his plate. He paused by the door long enough to aim a sympathetic glance in her direction.

Despite being curious about what they thought had happened, she didn't ask. Maybe they assumed she was upset because today she'd be handing over the job of caring for the Miller *kinder* to Juanita.

A terse laugh tickled her throat, but letting it escape would be a sure sign that there was something distressing going on between her and the Millers. Her family might suspect the truth, but to confirm it could cause the dam restraining Leanna's hot tears to collapse. Instead, she ate her breakfast and tried to pretend the morning was like any other.

As Leanna reached for her bonnet when breakfast was over, Juanita edged across the kitchen to stand in front of her. "You don't need to go with me this morning. I can go by myself."

"No, I told him that I'd show you around this morning."

"How difficult can it be? Gabriel and Michael have

a kitchen. We have a kitchen. They've got a washing machine. We've got a washing machine. They've got a clothesline. We do, too."

"He has two *bopplin*."

"I know that! I've played with them a bunch of times." Her younger sister stood with her hands on her hips and gave Leanna a frown she'd borrowed from their *grossmammi*. "What's wrong? Did you two have words after the graduation?"

"Don't be silly."

"I'm not being silly. You are. You looked thrilled to see Gabriel when he came into the school. After Harley choked, he took off, and you acted as if he'd never showed up at all."

Leanna didn't bother to correct her sister. Harley hadn't choked, and there was no possible way Leanna could ever be unaware of Gabriel.

"You were there, Juanita. You would have heard if we'd had words."

Except for the ones ricocheting through my head, and I don't know how to silence them. How can I ignore the truth that he wasn't honest—he was walking out with me and seeing Freda at the same time?

"I don't know what's going on, but I don't like you being glum and dreary," Juanita said with a childish stamp of her foot. "If you won't tell me what happened, I'll ask Gabriel."

"You—"

Grossmammi Inez's voice interrupted Leanna. Folding her arms over her chest, she said in a voice that grew more halting every day, "You will not, Juanita Wagler, stick your nose into matters that don't concern you. Yesterday you graduated from school into the adult world, so you need to start thinking like an adult instead of a scholar. Do I make myself clear?"

"Ja, Grossmammi." Juanita hung her head before opening the door and walking out.

Before Leanna could follow, the older woman said to the otherwise empty room, "It's wrong for Juanita to intrude, but it's as wrong for you to keep punishing yourself and Gabriel."

"I'm not punishing anyone." She wanted to add that she was the one suffering, but then she'd sound as immature as Juanita.

"I want you to ask yourself two things. First, are you following God's path or your own? Second, are you acting as you'd want others to act toward you?"

Leanna lowered her head, chastised. She knew the answer to the questions, and neither answer made her comfortable. Nothing was simple, a sure sign she'd wandered away from God's plan for her. When she'd first looked for work near Harmony Creek Hollow, everything had fallen into place so quickly that Leanna had no doubts God's hand had been in the changes. Even before she put the word out that she was looking for housecleaning jobs, three women had come to her asking if she was interested in working for them. Now she was returning to that work, and she should be grateful she had jobs where she enjoyed working for people she liked.

"Danki for making me think," she said, "instead of just being emotional."

"Our emotions are there to guide us, but sometimes we get so caught up in them they blind us to the truth. Don't forget that, Leanna."

"I won't." She gave her *grossmammi* a gentle hug, shocked anew at how much more fragile the older woman was with each passing day. The testing on

Grossmammi Inez's heart was scheduled for Thursday, and Leanna couldn't wait for results. Surely they would lead to a treatment to make her *grossmammi* feel better.

In spite of her determination to accept the future God had mapped out for her, Leanna was uneasy as she walked with her sister to the Millers' house. She was surprised but relieved when they got there that Gabriel had already left. Michael told them a lumber supply order had come in a day earlier than expected, and Gabriel had gone to make arrangements to have it delivered to their next work site on Archibald Street in Salem. They were repairing the porches on a house that had been built almost three centuries before.

Giving her sister a quick tour of the house, Leanna tried to think of what, if anything, she'd overlooked. "If you've got any other questions, ask. If I can't answer them, he will."

"*He* has a name, y'know," Juanita said in a petulant voice. It would take her sister some time to forgive Leanna for the conversation that had led to *Grossmammi* Inez scolding them.

"I know."

"How long are you going to avoid saying it?"

Leanna didn't reply. If she said she wasn't trying not to speak Gabriel's name, it might be a lie. She didn't know why she was calling him "he." It could be as simple as she wanted to keep some distance between her thoughts of him and her aching heart.

"I think I've told you everything you need to know," Leanna said as she looked around Gabriel's kitchen.

She'd explained to Juanita how the kitchen faucet had to be turned on slowly or it sprayed everywhere. She'd shown her younger sister which burner on the stove didn't work. The goats' *milch* formula was poured into bottles and waiting in the refrigerator. Fresh diapers and bibs were stacked on one end of the kitchen table.

"I've taken care of other *bopplin*, Leanna. We'll be fine."

"I know you will."

"Then go, or you'll be late. You know how Mrs. Duchamps gets annoyed if you don't get there on time."

Leanna struggled to smile. "It's because she worries something has happened. She can find a cloud around any silver lining. One time, she convinced herself I'd had a buggy accident and was lying beside the road near death because I wasn't there ten minutes early."

"You're babbling." Her younger sister made shooing motions with her hands. "Go, or you will have that nice old lady ready to call nine-one-one."

She bent to kiss the tops of the twins' heads. Their soft red hair tickled her nose, but she didn't feel like laughing. For more than two weeks, she'd spent most of her waking hours with them, and now she'd see them far less often. *Ja*, she could offer to bounce one of them on her knee during the long Sunday service. She might run into Gabriel and the *bopplin* along the twisting road through the hollow or at a store in the village. If she came over with fresh lemonade and sat on the porch with the Millers when they returned home at the end of the workday, it wouldn't be the same as spending each day with Heidi and Harley and watching how they grew and changed.

Without another word, she left and walked home. There, she hitched up the horse and drove to Mrs. Duchamps's house, which was the easternmost one in the village of Salem. Such a short time had passed since the last time she'd been there, but it seemed as if it'd been part of someone else's life. Someone who hadn't run into her past and had it implode around her.

Mrs. Duchamps answered the front door herself. She was a white-haired woman who towered over Leanna. She carried a cane, but she stood as straight as the spruce dominating her front lawn. Always dressing in bright colors, she collected whimsical bear figurines. She had hundreds, displayed on every flat surface in the house. As well, she had paintings of teddy bears hanging on the walls and a quilt with blue-and-green bears draped over her bed.

"It's good to have you back, Leanna." She stepped to one side, letting Leanna in.

"I'm glad to be here." That was the truth.

Or at least part of it.

At Mrs. Duchamps's house, she didn't have to judge each word she spoke before she let it past her lips. She could think of the present and not worry about what had happened in the past.

On the other hand, at Mrs. Duchamps's house, she wouldn't see the twins and marvel at their endless mischief and efforts to try something new. And she wouldn't have a chance to talk to Gabriel or see one of his rare smiles. Even when he annoyed her so much that she wanted to stamp her foot and demand that he listen to common sense, she'd enjoyed watching him with his *kinder*.

"You remember where everything is?" the elderly woman asked.

"*Ja*. I'll start in the upstairs bathroom as usual."

"Your sister started in the kitchen."

"Do you prefer that?" She hadn't guessed Juanita would make such a change from the routine Leanna had given her. What would her sister alter with the twins?

"Whatever works for you, dear."

Leanna nodded, but went into the kitchen instead of upstairs to the bathroom. She'd worked long enough for Mrs. Duchamps to recognize that any comment, even one that the elderly woman said wasn't important, was a suggestion that needed to be followed.

As she collected the cleaning supplies from the shelf where she'd stored them in the pantry so they were available when she came, she tried to focus on her job. It was impossible. Her mind was filled with confusion and sorrow. If someone else was in such a state, she would have urged them to talk to the person upsetting them.

What was the point of talking to Gabriel? She couldn't ask him point-blank the one question that preyed on her mind: Why had he spent time with her when he was having a more intimate relationship with Freda? Gabriel had walked out with Leanna for almost five months, so it wasn't as if he were on the rebound from breaking up with Freda. She didn't want to think she'd been wrong—now as well as months ago—when she'd believed he was a *gut* and decent man. Yet he must have married Freda after she became pregnant.

Pregnancies that happened before wedding vows were spoken weren't unheard-of in plain communities. In fact, the bishop who'd overseen their district had a daughter who'd anticipated her vows. The girl had asked for forgiveness and been granted it. She'd gone on to marry the man she loved.

Why had it been so easy to offer forgiveness to that young woman and impossible to offer the same to Gabriel? He must have atoned to his district's *Leit* before he'd been baptized and spoken his vows with Freda.

When *Grossmammi* Inez had been reading to them from the Bible each evening, she'd reminded them of the importance of forgiving one another. "To deny others what we have been given means that we're turning our faces and our lives away from God."

Leanna didn't want that, but she couldn't let go of her anger and betrayal, either. Scrubbing the tile floor so hard she threatened to rub the pattern right off the ceramic didn't help.

She didn't pause when a phone rang. Mrs. Duchamps's muffled voice drifted to her, and she looked up when the old woman peeked into the kitchen and said the caller had asked for Leanna.

Praying her *grossmammi* hadn't taken a turn for the worse, Leanna went into the living room where the phone was. She picked it up, listened and said, "I'll be there as soon as I can." She put the phone in its cradle. Seeing Mrs. Duchamps in the doorway, she said, "I need to go. It's an emergency."

Mrs. Duchamps rubbed her hands together. "What's wrong? Is someone ill? Changeable weather in the spring brings on colds and other worse things. Or did someone get injured? There are so many ways to be hurt on a farm. It isn't your grandmother, is it? She—"

Knowing that the elderly woman could go on and on, Leanna said, "It's my younger sister. She needs help with two *bopplin*—babies—she's watching for the first time."

"Are they okay?"

"They're going to be fine, I'm sure." She wasn't certain she could say the same for Juanita. It wasn't like her younger sister to panic. "Let me check on her, and then I'll come and finish up."

"Take as much time as you need."

"Danki." Leanna gave Mrs. Duchamps a stern look. "Don't touch that bucket. It's too heavy for you."

The old woman made a sweeping motion toward the door. "I won't touch it. I promise. Go and see what's wrong with those little ones."

A dozen possibilities ran through Leanna's head as she drove the buggy at the highest possible speed along the main road before turning onto the one following Harmony Creek. Racing past the camp where Mercy Stoltzfus planned to have city *kinder* come to spend a couple of weeks in the country with horses, she saw her friend Sarah's brother jump out of the way as the buggy rushed past. Benjamin shouted a question after her, but she didn't slow.

Apologizing to the horse as she jumped out of the buggy in front of the Millers' house, she ran to the door and flung it open.

Juanita whirled to face her. Remnants of tears on her sister's face matched those on the *bopplin*'s. "They stopped crying."

"When?"

"Right now." Juanita stared at her in amazement. "I heard your footsteps on the porch, so they must have, too. And then they stopped crying." She shook her head and snapped her fingers. "Just like that."

"Curiosity—"

"Has nothing to do with it. They recognized the sound of your steps. They don't want anything to do with me. They want you."

"They're *bopplin*. They want everything."

Juanita shook her head. "No, they didn't want anything but you. Nothing I tried would convince them to quit crying. As soon as you put a single toe on the porch, they stopped."

Knowing she wouldn't get anywhere arguing with

her sister when Juanita was so definite, Leanna squatted next to the *kinder*. *"Was iss letz, lieblings?"*

Of course, the twins didn't answer her and tell her what was wrong, but Heidi reached out and handed her one of the blocks she'd been clenching in her tiny hands.

Leanna didn't take it as she noticed Harley gasping for breath as he had the day before. She picked up the little boy and cuddled him. His uneven breathing eased, and some color returned to his face. When she held him up to her shoulder, his breaths, quick and shallow, brushed her neck. She murmured nonsense words until he calmed and wasn't shuddering with each inhalation.

He didn't cry much, she realized. She'd considered him the most content *boppli* she'd ever seen, but a sliver of worry pierced her mind. Could it be that he didn't cry because he'd come to realize how he struggled to breathe when he sobbed?

She couldn't ask a *boppli* such a question, but there was one she could ask her sister.

"Juanita, how did you call Mrs. Duchamps's house?"

With guilt blossoming on her face, her sister reached into a pocket under her apron and pulled out a cell phone.

"Where did you get that?" Leanna asked.

Her sister's cheeks grew bright red. "From Eugene. He got it because he's working in Salem with his uncle now that he's graduated from school."

"But why do you have it?" She made sure her voice was gentler, guessing her sister had a crush on Eugene Yoder.

"He thought I might need it on my first day of work here, and he was right, ain't so?"

Leanna started to answer, then halted when the back

door opened. As Gabriel walked in, her sister shoved the cell phone back into her pocket.

His hair was laced with sawdust, and a swath of dirt on the right side of his face emphasized his high cheekbones. "Leanna?" he asked, halting in midstep.

"Gute mariye," she said as if the past twenty-four hours hadn't happened. What *gut* would it do to rehash what had happened? She should be thinking of the *bopplin* and what was best for them.

"What are you doing here? I thought you had houses to clean today."

"I did. I mean, I do." She put Harley on the quilt. Getting a banana off the counter, she peeled and sliced it while she said, "Juanita couldn't stop the twins from crying, so she sent for me." There was no reason to bring the cell phone into the discussion. She handed each of the *bopplin* two pieces of the fruit.

"Are they okay?" He rushed to where his *kinder* were happily eating and making a mess with the banana. Looking at Leanna, he asked, "What happened?"

"Like I said, Juanita couldn't calm them. She called me to come and help."

"I see you've done that." His shoulders relaxed, and the wild expression of dismay faded. *"Danki,* Leanna, for helping."

"I'm glad I could." Smiling at her sister, she said, "It looks as if everything is under control. I need to get back to Mrs. Duchamps's house."

Gabriel walked with her out of the house, explaining he'd come to get some tools they hadn't realized they'd need this morning. "Mrs. Fenton keeps adding small details for the job, and Michael didn't have what he needed. When I got here and saw the buggy in the drive, I wanted to check what was going on."

"It doesn't seem to have been anything other than jitters from Juanita." She forced a smile. "I don't think there will be any other problems."

A shriek sent a shiver down her spine, and she spun to look at the house. Another followed. She heard Gabriel shout something, but didn't pay attention to his words as she rushed into the kitchen. As if someone had flipped a switch, the screaming stopped.

Tears rolled down small faces, and bananas were squashed between tiny fingers as the twins stared at her. Again Heidi held up her arms. Harley did as well, trying to lift himself off the floor as he did whenever he wanted her to pick him up. Beside them, Juanita looked as pale as fresh *milch*.

Coming to her feet at the same time Gabriel burst into the kitchen, Juanita raised her hands in a pose of surrender. "I told you. As soon as you leave, Leanna, they go into fire siren mode. As soon as you come back, they're okay again."

"I didn't expect this," Gabriel said.

"Me, either." Leanna knelt on the quilt. "This is a problem." She couldn't imagine leaving again when she knew Harley might choke again on his own sobs. "I don't know what's going on."

"They miss you." Juanita shrugged. "Well, it's true. They've never had a *mamm* that they remember, so you're the only *mamm* they've known. Isn't that right, Gabriel?"

Watching color drain from Leanna's face, Gabriel sighed. Once Juanita had spoken, it was obvious to him that the teenager had seen what he and Leanna had ignored. The *kinder* adored her. Not as a babysitter, but as a replacement for the *mamm* they'd never known.

"How old were the twins when your wife died?" asked Juanita when nobody else spoke.

"Five weeks old."

Both Waglers gasped at his answer.

"So young," murmured Leanna. "And such a short time with Freda."

"They were in the hospital for the first three weeks after they were born, but they seemed to be thriving," he said, staring out the window because he couldn't bear to look at Leanna when he revealed his part of the sad story. "I was so focused on them that I didn't notice Freda wasn't."

Leanna stood, but didn't move toward him. "I'm sorry, Gabriel."

"So what do we do for them?" he asked, desperate to change the subject to anything but his failure to see what Freda had needed. "Leanna has her jobs, and they're too young to understand they'll see her a lot less anyhow."

"I don't know." Leanna seemed about to add something more, but must have thought better of it.

"The answer is simple." Juanita gave them an easy smile.

Leanna frowned. "The answer to what is simple?"

"Making sure the *bopplin* don't work themselves into a tizzy as they have this morning."

"Go ahead," Gabriel said, though he had a *gut* idea what Juanita would say next.

"Leanna needs to take care of them while I do her cleaning jobs."

"Have you lost your mind?" asked Leanna in astonishment as she picked up Heidi and carried her to the sink to wash crushed banana off her hands.

"No, it's a brilliant idea." Juanita's grin broadened.

"What do you think, Gabriel? Doesn't it make sense for Leanna and me to switch jobs?"

He wanted to check and make sure his ears weren't clogged or had stopped working. Or was it his brain that wasn't functioning?

"Switch jobs?" he repeated. "Are you saying Leanna would stay as the babysitter for the twins?"

"And she'd take over my cleaning jobs." Leanna didn't look at him.

Juanita did, though, and she was smiling with delight at what she thought was a simple solution. "So what do you say, Gabriel? Are you okay with it?"

Okay? He was torn between jumping up and down with gratitude or shouting out that it was the stupidest idea that had ever been conceived. Nothing he was experiencing at that moment was as tepid as an *okay*.

"If we take a week or two and wean them off my being here all day each day," Leanna said, "then they should be fine with Juanita."

"It's worth a try." He ignored how his heart did a dance at the thought of seeing her each morning and evening. "Will your cleaning clients agree?"

"They have so far," Juanita interjected. "If everyone here is fine with this, I should get over to Mrs. Duchamps's house and finish up, Leanna."

With a weary wave, Leanna motioned for her to go.

Why hadn't he thought how tough this was for Leanna, too? He'd seen her face when Michael blurted out about the twins' upcoming birthday. She had figured out that Freda was pregnant when they took their vows, but without knowing the whole story, Leanna could only assume he'd cheated on her while they were walking out together.

If only Aden hadn't asked him to promise not to reveal the truth—

He silenced the thought before it could play out in his mind. "I'm sorry for making things difficult for you."

"I know, but we'll work this out."

Was that an acceptance of his apology? He doubted she had any idea how much he craved her forgiveness.

And how is she supposed to offer that when you haven't been honest with her?

He'd lost count of the number of times that question had rippled through his mind, but he knew how many times he'd answered it.

Not once.

Chapter Twelve

When Leanna walked into the bustling Salem Volunteer Fire Department building on Saturday morning, she couldn't utter a single word. Her throat clogged with tears of gratitude when she saw the long line of people waiting to check in for the blood drive that was being held in honor of *Grossmammi* Inez, though it wasn't certain yet that *Grossmammi* Inez would have to have surgery. Several of the men in the *Leit*, including Miriam's husband and brother, were volunteer firefighters who'd helped arrange it.

Her *grossmammi* had protested being singled out, but their minister had assured her it was common practice to give the blood drive a human face. Eli had added that was important because it brought in more people to donate the pints of blood that were always in short supply. At that, *Grossmammi* Inez had relented.

Leanna had entered the firehouse from the back and walked through the multipurpose room. She'd been there before for fund-raising suppers. At those, folding tables and chairs had been arranged the length of the room, and the firefighters, along with the volunteer EMTs, had been busy in the kitchen area. Today they were checking people in and escorting them to where they could wait on chairs in neat rows in the bay where the ambulance usually parked. In the neighboring area, the spot where the pumper was stored, screens divided the gurneys where volunteers were already donating pints of blood.

She recognized many of the volunteer firefighters who were assisting the blood bank personnel. Not only her plain neighbors, but *Englischers* who'd participated in events with the fire department. Some of them had worked at a mud sale earlier in the spring. She was sure she recognized the tall, mustached man. He had served as the auctioneer who'd sold the quilt she'd donated.

She waved to Sarah. Her friend had taken the rigorous training last fall and was now the first plain female volunteer EMT. She didn't wear trousers and T-shirts as the others did, but she'd put masking tape across the front of her black apron and written the words "blood drive volunteer" on it.

Sarah hurried over, her red hair aglow in the bright lights hanging from metal beams across the ceiling. "I was wondering when you'd get here. The volunteers from the blood service have been looking forward to meeting someone from your family."

"Isn't Lyndon here already?" Her older brother was an enthusiastic volunteer firefighter.

"I haven't seen him."

Leanna rolled her eyes. "I forgot. He had to go to Greenwich to pick up a part for his baler. He figured he could get there and back without missing too much of the blood drive."

"*Komm mol*, and I'll introduce you around."

"I want to donate, too."

"Don't worry. We won't let you leave until you've

got a pint less of blood inside you." Hooking her arm through Leanna's, she led her to the first table.

Leanna thanked the volunteers while she was being signed in and answering a health questionnaire. When she was shown to a gurney, she stretched out on it and followed the instructions given to her by a young *Englischer*. He asked questions about her *grossmammi* while he inserted the needle. He laughed when Leanna told him one of her favorite stories about *Grossmammi* Inez.

She'd been with the elderly woman a few years ago when they came across a skunk in the road. *Grossmammi* Inez had put her hands on her waist, given the skunk a stern look and said in the same tone she used with her *kins-kinder* when they were misbehaving, "If you know what's *gut* for you, skunk, you'll get out of here. Now!"

Chuckling, Leanna said, "And the wildest thing is that the skunk waddled off as if it'd understood her. Didn't send a bit of nasty scent our way."

"I guess we all learn to listen to our grandparents," the young man said. "Even skunks." He put tape over the needle to hold it and the IV in place.

"That hardly hurt," Leanna said as he handed her a soft rubber ball shaped like a bright red heart to squeeze while the blood pumped into the donation bag. "I've pricked myself worse when I'm quilting."

"Glad to hear it. Call for me if you need anything or if you feel woozy."

"Woozy? Is that a medical term?"

He laughed. "One of the first they teach us in nursing school."

Leaning back on the raised head of the table while she watched her blood ooze through the clear tube, she thanked God for the wisdom that had allowed medical professionals to know how to save lives with donated blood.

Less than a half hour later, Leanna sat at a small table enjoying some orange juice and chocolate chip and dried cranberry cookies that had been donated by the bakery where her twin worked. She smiled when Annie joined her, a small piece of gauze taped to the inside of her arm.

"Your cookies are delicious as always," Leanna said.

"Not mine. Those are Caleb's recipe. He's always trying something new." Annie's nose, so like her own, crinkled. "Ask him sometime about the peanut-butter-and-banana cookies he tried making. Ask. Don't try one!"

"I'll keep that in mind."

"What a great turnout!" Annie's grin returned. "Wait until *Grossmammi* Inez hears about this."

"She won't have to hear about it," replied a deeper voice from behind Leanna. "Not when she can see it with her own two eyes."

Whirling in her chair, Leanna gaped at the sight of her *grossmammi*, weak but as determined as ever, standing with one hand on her cane and the other on Gabriel's arm.

"*Grossmammi* Inez!" she gasped.

Everyone in the room seemed to turn at once and stare at the four of them. Volunteers rushed forward to greet her *grossmammi*. The older woman acted unabashed by the attention. She turned every comment into grateful words to each person who came up to thank her for being a part of the blood drive. She was urged to sit at the table. A fresh cup of *kaffi* appeared from somewhere, along with a plate topped by a generous selection of Caleb's cookies.

Leanna stood quickly. Too quickly, because her head spun and the room seemed to telescope in on itself. Determined, she blinked to bring everything into focus as she stepped aside to let others have a chance to speak with her *grossmammi*.

She grabbed Gabriel's arm and motioned with her head for him to follow her away from the crowd. As soon as she guessed they were out of anyone else's earshot, she said, "She shouldn't be here. The *doktor* wants her to avoid people so she doesn't pick up some bug that could do more damage to her heart."

"I didn't plan to bring her, so don't be angry with me." He raised his hands in a pose of surrender. "She flagged me down when I was driving past. If I hadn't agreed to bring her, she would have walked."

With a sigh, Leanna had to admit that Gabriel was right. Her *grossmammi* had been upset that her faulty heart valve was keeping her from visiting neighbors as she'd done the previous spring.

"Where are the twins?"

He pointed to a small door to the right. "There's a room set up as a nursery. I left them there with a few other *kinder*. I should get in line to donate, too."

"Gabriel?"

"Ja?"

"I'm sorry that I jumped to conclusions about you bringing *Grossmammi* Inez here."

"It's okay. I know you've gotten used to assuming the worst of me."

"I…" She wanted to deny his words, but she couldn't. "I'll try to change that."

He looked surprised. "You've got every right to believe as you do after what's happened between us."

"Living in the past means not treasuring gifts of the future. *Grossmammi* Inez has said that more times than I can count."

"Your *grossmammi* is a smart woman."

"I agree."

When he took her hand and squeezed it gently, she almost gasped. He strode away to go through the process of donating, and she stared at him. Had he meant to give her some sort of message by holding her hand?

If so, she didn't have any idea what he'd meant to tell her.

Leanna joined the other volunteers and passed out glasses of juice and cookies to people who'd donated blood. When the *Englisch* donors saw her plain clothing, they asked about her *grossmammi*, and she shared more stories about *Grossmammi* Inez with them. She was touched by their solicitousness for a woman they'd never met before today.

When Michael sat at one of the tables, she smiled. She handed him some juice and offered him a choice of cookies. At the same time, she glanced around the firehouse. She didn't see Gabriel, so he must be behind one of the screens in the donation area.

Thanking her for the three cookies he took, Michael said, "I've been wanting to see the inside of the firehouse, and this was my first chance." He gave her a teasing wink. "I didn't think it would cost me a pint of blood."

"*Danki* for coming today."

"It's the least I can do for your *grossmammi*, who has sent over so many delicious meals to us."

"We've been happy to help."

"And we've been happy that you've been happy to help." He gave a weak smile. "Is it usual for me to be seeing double?"

She glanced over her shoulder, hoping to see Annie. Her twin was nowhere in sight, either. "Let me call one of the nurses."

He rested his elbow on the table and leaned his head against his open palm. Tilting his head so he could see her, he said, "No, don't bother them. I was in a hurry to get up. I should have waited a few more minutes as they told me to do."

"I can still check with one of the nurses for you."

"Don't bother." He closed his eyes. "Gabriel promised me if I came and donated, he'd make sure I got home if he had to strap me to the back of the buggy."

She laughed. "I'd like to see that."

"Oh, you will." He opened one eye. "My brother never breaks a promise, which is why he's so leery of making them."

"You've said that before."

His brow furrowed. "Because it's true. I don't know what promise he made before he got married, but he changed after he told me that he'd decided to marry Freda."

Leanna murmured something about him resting. She wasn't sure herself what she said, but Michael nodded and shut his eyes again. After backing away from the table, she set the plate next to others. She walked toward the room where the older *kinder* were, she'd been told, being entertained by one of the teachers from the public school while the younger *kinder* played with simple toys.

If anyone spoke to her, she didn't hear them. If someone was in her way, they must have stepped aside before she bumped into them because she was lost in her swirling thoughts.

Gabriel had changed so much, though he was again smiling and occasionally laughing. She'd assumed he'd grown grim after Freda's death, but Michael's comment suggested otherwise. Why hadn't he been happy when he married Freda? She was the *mamm* of his *kinder*. He must have loved her, so why hadn't he been happy Freda had agreed to become his wife?

It was another question she couldn't ask, but for the first time, she wasn't sure she wanted to satisfy her curiosity. She feared knowing the truth would change her as much as it had Gabriel.

Leaving the busy donation area, Gabriel looked around. Had Leanna gone home already? He saw her *grossmammi* and her siblings other than Lyndon talking with volunteers and donors. As he thought about Leanna's brother, Lyndon rushed in to be teased by his fellow firefighters, who thought it was hilarious he was late for the blood drive held for his own *grossmammi*.

A surge of gratitude washed over Gabriel as he watched the camaraderie among the *Leit* and the *Englischers*. In the small town, they were dependent upon each other in so many ways, though the plain people kept most of their daily lives separate from their neighbors. He'd hoped their new home would be like this when he accepted Caleb Hartz's invitation to purchase the run-down farm not far from Caleb's own place along Harmony Creek.

What would have happened if he and Freda had lived here instead of Lancaster County? A few gossips there had stuck their noses into everyone's business, carrying tales, whether they were true or not, to the bishop who always took them at their word, even when it caused divisions in the district. That had been one of the reasons Gabriel had jumped at the chance to begin over again in northern New York.

Would Aden have feared so much for his daughter and the family's reputation if they'd been living among these people, instead? Not that the *Leit* in Harmony Creek Hollow or the others in Salem were perfect. No one on earth was, but he'd seen the way his plain neighbors had accepted one another's mistakes with kindness and supported each other through the difficult phase of re-creating lives in a new place laced with so many hopes and dreams.

Not seeing Leanna anywhere, he headed for the nursery. Soon it would be time for the twins' dinner, and he should get them home. He enjoyed sharing the midday meal with the *bopplin* on the weekends because during the week he didn't have the opportunity.

He entered the room and smiled. Leanna sat on the floor next to the twins, who were cuddled as close to her as they could. The *kinder* adored her, and he understood why. She never attempted to hide how much she loved Heidi and Harley. She'd brought them two of the heart-shaped balls used in the donation area. Both *bopplin* giggled when they squeezed the bright red balls. With a laugh of her own, Leanna guided the ball Heidi held away from the little girl's mouth.

Wrinkling her nose, she said, "Yucky. It's yucky."

"Ya-ya," Heidi parroted back.

Gabriel chuckled when she tried to copy Leanna's expression and ended up crossing her eyes, instead.

Leanna looked up and smiled. It seemed forced, but

he wasn't going to remark on that. Still, he wondered why she wasn't wearing her customary bright expression.

"We're playing 'let's not eat the ball,'" she said.

"How do you play it?" He sat on the other side of the twins.

"Heidi and Harley try to eat the balls, and I try to keep them from doing so."

"Pretty simple rules."

"Yet it's not as easy as it sounds."

"So I see." He reached across the space between them. Tapping Heidi's nose, he grinned when she managed to scrunch up her own nose.

The *boppli* chortled and raised the ball high above her red curls before bringing it down on her knee. She repeated the motion over and over, her delight visible to everyone who walked past.

"Watch out!" Leanna warned. "Harley wants to take a bite out of his!"

Putting his fingers on the ball the little boy held, Gabriel lowered it away from his lips.

Harley opened his mouth to protest, but became fascinated when Gabriel guided his arms in the same up-and-down pattern as his sister.

"Danki," Leanna said. "I was beginning to wonder if God would listen to my prayer to send someone to help or to give me a couple of extra hands so I could keep them from eating the balls. Clearly today, Gabriel, you're the answer to my prayer."

"I'm not that." Her words made him uncomfortable.

Not that she meant them as anything other than a cheerful remark, but each one reminded him of how he'd broken her heart.

"Why not? I prayed for help, and here you are. Don't you believe God hears our prayers and answers them?"

He jerked at the feeling as if she'd driven a knife into him, draining away his contentment with playing with the *kinder.* "Do *you* believe that?"

"*Ja,* with every bit of my heart."

"I wish I could."

"Why can't you?"

He met her eyes over the *bopplin'*s heads. "Because, assuming God heard my prayers, He hasn't answered them."

Plucking the ball out of Heidi's mouth again, she said, "If you're talking about when Freda and her *daed* died, you know that our prayers aren't always answered in the way we want them to be. We can't see what God knows."

"I know that, Leanna."

"You don't believe it." She reached past the twins to jab a finger into his chest. "Not here."

"I prayed for Freda and Aden to be freed from their pain." He held up a hand. "Don't tell me that God answered my prayer because He took their pain away when they died."

"No, I won't tell you that. God knows what was in your heart. And it wasn't that you wished to lose two people who were so important to you. Let Him into your heart, Gabriel, and He'll show you the truth of His love."

"I don't know how to take down the wall between me and Him."

"The same way you built it, but in reverse." She gave him a sympathetic smile. "You're a builder. You know how these things work. It's harder sometimes to take down a wall than to put it up, because you must be careful and pay attention to every step you take."

"You make it sound easy."

"No, I don't. I know how hard it is."

"Do you? Really?" He folded his arms in front of him and frowned.

"*Ja*, I've gotten angry at God, too. I ran away from everything I knew, too."

"When was that?"

"When you married Freda and I had the chance to move here." She stood, turned on her heel and walked away, not giving him a chance to reply.

What could he have said?

If only Aden hadn't asked him to promise not to reveal the truth that would hurt his daughter in the eyes of the community...

Chapter Thirteen

Leanna stopped at the bottom of the stairs in Gabriel's house the following Tuesday morning and held her breath as she listened for the *kinder*. Not a sound. She shouldn't be surprised. The twins had been more than ready for their nap when she put them down about ten minutes ago. Gabriel had warned her that Heidi and Harley had been up late last night because Benjamin and Menno Kuhns had come over to discuss having the Millers use some of their lumber in upcoming construction projects. The conversation had gone on, and Gabriel hadn't had a chance to put the *bopplin* to bed until after Sarah's brothers had left.

She was glad to hear about the two sets of brothers doing business together. She'd heard Michael complain more than once that the lumberyard where they'd been getting their supplies wasn't as dependable as he was accustomed to in Pennsylvania. Knowing how dedicated the Kuhns brothers were, she guessed they'd have the proper lengths of wood at a job site at the exact time Gabriel and Michael needed them.

She went into the kitchen and opened the bag she'd brought with her along with her regular satchel containing the *bopplin*'s bottles of formula. She pulled out long rubber gloves and plastic protective glasses, as well as her soap molds. She'd asked Gabriel last night before she left if she could make soap today if the twins napped long enough. The task was simpler when there weren't other people around.

Simpler and safer, because the lye she used was caustic. She usually made the soap when her younger siblings and Lyndon's *kinder* were in school. With school out for the summer, it'd be easier at Gabriel's house.

She was surprised when Gabriel walked in right after she'd finished measuring and melting lard, coconut oil and canola oil. He went to the refrigerator and pulled out the pitcher of ice tea she'd made earlier.

Pouring a glass, he asked, "Do you want one?"

"Not until I'm done making soap." She gestured with her elbow. "Please stay back."

"Mind if I sit at the table and watch? I've never seen anyone make soap before. I'll stay out of your way so I won't do anything to distract you."

"All right," she replied. Didn't he realize that his presence was distracting? "I thought you'd be out all afternoon."

"Michael is at the job site. I went to the livestock auction in Cambridge."

Measuring the temperature of the oils with a hand-held thermometer, she asked, "Did you buy anything?"

"A small herd of dairy cows. They'll be delivered in a couple of days. Once they're here, I can start milking the half dozen that are giving *milch*, though I'll have to buy some feed for them until I can get a full crop in and harvested next year. The grass in the pasture is growing well, and I should be able to get a first cutting by the end of the month."

The anticipation in his voice made her smile, but she didn't turn as she retrieved her frozen goats' *milch* packets from where she'd stored them in the freezer. As she chopped the *milch* into chunks and put it in a large metal bowl, she said, "It's what you've been waiting for, ain't so?"

"*Ja.* This is the next step in building a future for my family on this farm. The land here needs work to make the soil as productive as it could be, but that will come in time."

"And soon the twins will be scurrying around trying to help and getting in your way while you milk."

Her hope that he'd laugh was dashed, but he did say, "I want them to learn everything about farming so they can appreciate what we have here as much as I do."

Leanna didn't answer as she pulled on her protective gloves and goggles. Measuring out the lye, she began to sprinkle it over the top of the frozen *milch*. She stirred between each small amount. The *milch* began to melt as she added more lye.

"Why do you have the *milch* frozen?" he asked. "Wouldn't it be simpler to have it liquid and pour it into the lye?"

"The lye has to go into the *milch*, not the other way around. If I put the lye in first, it'd erupt like a volcano." She kept adding in small amounts of lye and stirring. "Having the *milch* frozen keeps it from curdling when I put in the lye."

He remained silent until she was finished with the lye and had poured in the melted oils. She put in a small amount of oatmeal and a few drops of lavender oil. Using a battery-operated handheld blender, she carefully mixed the ingredients, making sure no bubbles appeared. Again and again she paused and lifted the blender out of the soap. Once the pattern of the blade remained visible, she ladled the soap into the molds, taking care not to drop any on the counter.

She gathered up the bowls. She made sure the lye container was closed before she put it in her bag.

When she'd finished cleaning her equipment and the counter, Gabriel poured her a glass of ice tea and refilled his own.

"Danki," she said, taking the glass and sitting at the table. "And *danki* for letting me use your kitchen to make soap today."

"It was fascinating." He sat facing her. "Do you always put in the same scents and the oatmeal?"

"Not always. Sometimes I use coffee grounds instead of oatmeal."

"Coffee grounds?"

"With them, I have a soap that exfoliates dry skin."

He held up his work-hardened hands. "Maybe I should try some?"

"I can bring you a bar in about a month because the soap has to cure."

"I had no idea that making soap was such a long process."

She smiled. "That's because the only parts of the process most people are familiar with are picking a packaged bar off the shelf and unwrapping it before using it."

"So why do you go to all this work?"

"Why are you working with Benjamin and Menno to make sure you have boards that meet your specifications?"

"Answering a question with a question is the sign of trying to avoid giving an answer."

"Why would I do that?"

"Why not?"

She laughed. This time, she was sure he was teasing her as he used to do.

Before he married Freda…

Leanna stood and walked away. While she'd been working at the counter, she'd had to focus on the soap. That had allowed her to forget, for a few precious minutes, about how Gabriel had been with Freda at the same time he'd been taking Leanna for buggy rides.

Now that she was over her initial shock at the realization of Freda being pregnant before marrying Gabriel, something didn't feel right to Leanna. Everything else she'd ever seen or heard about him proclaimed he was an honest man. If he'd been spending time with Freda, he would have said something to Leanna. Even if he'd been determined to keep it a secret, why hadn't she heard the truth from someone else? Others had ended up with their names repeated along the Amish grapevine when they had stopped or started walking out with someone new. It was an illusion nobody knew who was courting whom. The truth was it was rare for anyone to be surprised when a marriage announcement was published during a church service.

Gabriel cleared his throat. How long had she been lost in her thoughts?

"I'm sorry," she said. "My mind was wandering."

"No, I should be the one saying I'm sorry. I know I've been gruff."

"An understatement."

"Again you're right."

Why was it so easy for her to accept his apology now but not be able to forgive him for breaking her heart? She should be eager to put the past behind her so she could move on.

Instead, the question of how long he'd been seeing

Freda while he was walking out with Leanna tried to slip past her lips. Again she kept the words from bursting forth. She should get his late wife out of her mind. Would it help if they spoke about Freda more? She'd seen him clamp his lips closed when someone mentioned his wife's name.

"Gabriel, we need to be straightforward with each other," she said.

Wariness narrowed his eyes. "What do you mean?"

She wanted to ask why he was looking at her as if he expected her to attack him at any moment. "I'm not sure how to act around you. I don't want to do anything to put more pressure on you. You put enough on yourself with getting the farm started, helping your brother, worrying about your *bopplin* and recovering from your wife's death. That's on top of having a wife become ill in the wake of the twins' being born, as well as a dying *daed*-in-law. That would be awful for anyone."

"I appreciate that, Leanna, but I'm fine."

"You may think so, but I know how difficult it is to have someone you love fall ill. When I was a *kind*, my *daed* died after being sick for what seemed like forever. I saw what my *mamm* went through nursing him. It took her a long time to recover her own health after that."

"I told you. I'm fine." His tone was as caustic as the lye she'd used. For a moment, she thought his bitterness was aimed at her, and then realized it wasn't. "Leanna, can we change the subject? This is too hard to talk about."

"It's okay to admit that it was hard. We *kinder* depended on Mamm during that time, too. We were older than the twins, so I can understand how tough it was for you as she got sicker and weaker and you had to do more for her. Trust me. I do understand, and I think it'd be *gut* for you to talk to someone who understands."

* * *

Gabriel's hands clenched on the table. "You don't understand a thing, Leanna! I didn't do a single thing for her. I didn't know how sick she was until she killed herself by overdosing on sleeping pills."

Leanna blanched as she gripped the edge of the counter. "Freda killed herself?"

He berated himself for opening that door to the past he'd fought to keep closed. "I wish you could forget that I said that." He shook his head and drew in a deep breath. His heart seemed to ache more with each beat, but at the same time a weight that had been grinding down into it had lessened at the exact moment he shared the truth.

His hands fisted more tightly. If he'd relieved an ounce of his suffering, it shouldn't have been because he'd passed it to Leanna. She'd stepped up to help him when she had every reason not to, and shifting his pain and grief to her couldn't be the way he repaid her.

"I can't forget it," she whispered, "but I won't say anything to anyone else."

"Danki."

"I'm so sorry." She put her hand on top of his clenched one. "You're right. I don't understand what you've gone through, but I hope that God will show me a way to help you."

With a raw growl that came from the depths of his throat, he shook his head. "Don't you think I've asked God for help? Go ahead and try it yourself if you want. Maybe you'll get a better response than I did, which was nothing."

"Tell me what happened."

"Are you sure you want to know?"

She was still for so long that he wasn't sure if she was going to reply. Finally she said, *"Ja."*

He stood, unable to sit and face her while he recounted what had happened. Staring out the window, he said, "Freda never seemed to recover from the twins' birth. After they were born, she didn't want to pump her *milch* for them. She complained when the nurses urged her to do so. I thought once she got home, things would be better. When she was home and the *bopplin* at the hospital, she moped. I thought she missed them, but she never wanted to go and see them. I spoke with the *doktor*, and he said having two *bopplin* as a first pregnancy was extra rough." He rubbed his uneven beard, then jerked his hand away from the thing that identified him as a widower. "I listened to him, because he'd been right about everything else. He'd been recommended to us, and he took such *gut* care of Freda during what was a difficult pregnancy."

"He was wrong about this," she whispered.

Her voice touched the chafed parts of his soul that had never healed. Instead of the pain he expected, her compassion offered a cooling balm. "*Ja*, he was wrong, but so was I. When Freda had a bad day, I'd try to re-assure her that things would get better as the *bopplin* grew and slept through the night. When she had a *gut* day, I convinced myself it meant the dark days were going to be over soon."

He'd failed Freda by not doing what his gut told him was the right thing. Instead, he'd let her convince him that seeing her *doktor* wouldn't help her. She told him time would bring healing.

She'd been lying to him, and he hadn't suspected.

That ate at him, though he didn't blame Freda. She'd been ill. He should have insisted she get care so he didn't have to come home and find her dead next to empty pill bottles and the picture of an *Englischer*. He should have been a stronger husband and put his foot down, taking her to the *doktor*. He'd failed her as the *daed* of her *kinder* had. Guilt swelled over him like a fever, hot and weakening him.

He took a deep breath and held it before exhaling. His guilt belonged to him and him alone. He couldn't dump it on Leanna. She didn't deserve that, though, he argued with himself, she deserved to know what type of man he truly was.

"And you came home," Leanna softly from right behind him, "to discover the *bopplin* howling and got no answer when you called to Freda." She put her hand on his back and leaned her forehead against his shoulder. "No wonder you reacted as you did the day you rushed upstairs here. I'm sorry to have made you go through that again. I had no idea."

"I know you didn't. You want me to be honest? Okay, I'll be honest. I don't want to risk my heart like that again. Not ever."

"But…" Her voice trailed away as a thin cry came from upstairs. It was followed by a louder one, an announcement that the twins were awake.

Leanna pushed away from him and hurried into the other room. As she reached the bottom of the stairs, she paused. She looked at him. Tears were luminous in her eyes.

"I understand why you don't want to chance suffering any more sorrow," she said in a broken voice.

In horror, he stared as she rushed up the stairs. She thought he'd been talking about falling in love with her. Was that what he'd meant? He wasn't sure.

Of anything any longer.

He took a step to follow, then halted. If he gave chase, what could he do but hurt her—the one person he had never wanted to hurt—more?

Chapter Fourteen

Leanna became aware of how her family was avoiding getting in her way when she stamped around the kitchen while she helped prepare supper that evening. It was as if she had an invisible cloud of silence around her and nobody was allowed to intrude. She also noticed she was chopping onions for a salad as if trying to drive the knife through the cutting board, the counter and right down to the floor.

She hadn't thought she could become any angrier at Gabriel than she'd been the day she'd found out he was marrying Freda Girod.

She'd been wrong.

When he'd told her that Freda had committed suicide, she'd offered sympathy with all her heart. He'd taken it, or at least he'd seemed to before he told her he wasn't ever going to risk his heart on another relationship.

But he never said he was ever in love with you.

She wished she could silence that thought, repeating in her mind like Heidi's endless nonsense words. Every thought, no matter how she tried to halt it, led her to Gabriel and his *kinder.* It'd been barely more than a month since he'd shown up by the pen where she kept her goats. Before that, she'd been sure she was on the road to forgetting how much he'd wounded her. Seeing his handsome face had swept aside all progress—albeit slight progress—that she'd made.

Leanna tried to focus, but it was impossible. Every motion felt as sharp as the knife she was using. During supper, the efforts her family made to act as if everything was normal seemed to emphasize how much was wrong in her life. She tried to participate in their conversations, but she couldn't seem to swim through the swamp of her thoughts and concentrate on what everyone else was saying.

At the end of a supper she hadn't tasted, Leanna offered to do the dishes because her twin was planning to take a walk with Caleb. Her younger siblings were so tired they could barely keep their eyes open, and she didn't want her *grossmammi* to help.

However, *Grossmammi* Inez remained at the table while Leanna washed and dried the dishes and cleaned up the kitchen. Other than the clatter of plates and cooking pots, the only sound in the room was her *grossmammi*'s labored breathing. Leanna considered urging her *grossmammi* to go to her bedroom and rest, but a single glance in the older woman's direction was enough for Leanna to know that *Grossmammi* Inez wasn't going to retire until she'd said what she had to say to Leanna.

"Would you like some more *milch*?" Leanna asked.

"That would be nice to sip on while we chat."

She poured a glass and carried it to the table. She set it in front of her *grossmammi* and sat beside her.

"Was iss letz?" *Grossmammi* Inez asked after taking a sip.

Though Leanna wanted to say "everything was wrong," she answered, "To begin with, I'm worried about you."

"You've been worried about me for weeks." Her *grossmammi* waved aside Leanna's words. "Something else is wrong. *Was iss letz?*"

Knowing she was wasting time by equivocating, she said, "I'm upset with Gabriel."

"I guessed that. You've been upset with him for longer than you've worried about me, but tonight's the first time you've tried to saw through the counter." After sipping again, she said, "Don't make me ask a lot of questions to persuade you to be honest with me, *kins-kind*, when I sound like an old train engine running out of steam. Just tell me what happened."

Leanna explained why she was upset with Gabriel, though she said nothing about Freda's suicide. She couldn't break the promise she'd made to Gabriel such a short time ago. When she ran out words, she closed her eyes so the tears searing her eyes wouldn't fall.

She waited for her *grossmammi*'s advice, but *Grossmammi* Inez didn't answer right away. Was it because she wanted to gather her thoughts, or did she need to fill her lungs with enough oxygen to let her to say what was already on her mind?

At last, *Grossmammi* Inez spoke. Her words were punctured by her gasps for breath, but that couldn't lessen the impact of what she said as she met Leanna's eyes.

"My dear *kins-kind*, do you want me to say it's okay for you to punish Gabriel for marrying someone else?"

"No!"

"Then you must be trying to punish yourself, because you continue to care about him after the greatest betrayal you've ever suffered." Compassion warmed her wrinkled face. "Is that what you plan to do with your life? Are you upset with him—and with yourself—

because you let yourself hope he'd turn to you and you could decide together what your futures would be?"

She was about to reply, then halted herself. Could *Grossmammi* Inez be right?

At last, Leanna said, "It's not my place to decide the future."

"*Gut.* I'm glad you're seeing sense before you destroy the kitchen."

Leanna smiled in spite of her aching heart. She was blessed to have her *grossmammi* to keep her on an even keel by reminding her of the need for faith in the One who held the future in His hands.

"I don't think it would have been all of the kitchen," she replied. "Maybe a quarter."

Grossmammi Inez patted Leanna's arm. "As it never happened, let's forget it."

"I owe you and the rest of the family an apology for being so self-absorbed."

"I know they would appreciate hearing that as much as I do." She smiled. "I know they will forgive you as I already have. And they *do* understand. All of us have had rough days."

She almost asked if any of her family had endured a day like she had with the news of Freda's suicide. The thought of her *grossmammi*'s grief when Leanna's parents died halted her. *"Danki, Grossmammi."*

After lifting her glass, the older woman drank deeply before she lowered it to the table. "Two of the most important verses to us plain people are in the sixth chapter of Matthew. Verses fourteen and fifteen. You know those verses, ain't so?"

"Ja."

"They are?"

Leanna said, "'For if ye forgive men their trespasses,

your Heavenly Father will also forgive you: But if ye forgive not men their trespasses, neither will your Father forgive your trespasses.'"

"Don't you think it's time you forgave Gabriel?"

"I've tried!"

"I know you have, and I'm glad that you haven't offered lip service to forgiving him in order to placate your conscience. Forgiveness that doesn't come from the heart isn't true forgiveness. But, Leanna, you need to search your heart and find a way to forgive him. Otherwise, you won't ever be free of the anger that has betrayed you today."

Leanna stared at her *grossmammi* in astonishment. Her anger had betrayed her? If asked, she would have said today's betrayal had come from Gabriel. Yet he hadn't done anything except to be honest with her as she'd asked him to. He'd been honest with her. Did she want him to spare her feelings by deceiving her?

No!

"Let me give you another set of verses to pray with tonight before you go to sleep," her *grossmammi* said as she pushed herself to her feet. "I've found they help me when someone doesn't meet my expectations, and I'm hurt. This is from *Psalms* 55: 'As for me, I will call upon God; and the Lord shall save me. Evening, and morning, and at noon, will I pray, and cry aloud: and He shall hear my voice. He hath delivered my soul in peace from the battle that was against me: for there were many with me.'" She put her hand over Leanna's. "Sometimes our battles are with others. Sometimes they are with ourselves."

Her *grossmammi* leaned forward to kiss Leanna's cheek before she moved out of the kitchen, leaving Leanna with thoughts whirling like a tornado.

* * *

Gabriel put down his pen on Thursday evening and rubbed his eyes as he looked across the kitchen, which was lit by a single propane lamp. His brother was out, visiting the Kuhns brothers. Michael and Benjamin were becoming *gut* friends, and Gabriel suspected they might go into business together while Gabriel concentrated on the farm.

The farm…

He almost groaned as he picked up the page of estimated expenses he'd compiled for the next six months. He and Michael had found enough work to pay their bills this month, even with the extra cost for the cows delivered that afternoon. He hoped he hadn't made a big mistake by starting a herd now. Next month, the budget must include money to pay for the cows' upkeep, as well as household expenses. The twins had another visit to the pediatrician in a few days, and though the fee for the last month's visit, including medicine for Heidi's ear infection, had been lower than he'd expected, it had been enough to put a burden on their budget.

"Not that you're a burden, little girl," he said as he glanced down at where she sat banging two wooden blocks together. "Or you, either, little man." He smiled at Harley, who was watching his sister.

Both *bopplin* grinned at him, and his heart swelled with love. He was blessed by having these two *kinder* in his life. That was something he'd never regret. What would Leanna think if he could tell her the truth about why he'd married Freda?

His lips tightened, and he put the budget page on the stack of papers in front of him. He needed to keep Leanna out of his head. She'd invaded his thoughts more than usual—though he hadn't guessed that could be possible—since he'd told her about Freda's death two days ago.

He sat back in his chair and stared at the ceiling where shadows moved in rhythm with the propane flame. Everything had changed, but nothing had. Leanna had come downstairs with the twins that afternoon when he'd arrived home, and she had made sure they were fed before she left for home. She'd returned the past two mornings, acting as if he'd never said a single word about Freda. She was kind and smiled, but he couldn't miss how her face seemed shadowed by sadness. She hadn't once met his eyes during their short conversations before he left for work and when he returned at day's end.

Yet she seemed to be keeping her promise. As far as he knew, she hadn't said a word about Freda's death, not even to him.

That hadn't surprised him, but he'd expected in the past two days she'd mention something—anything—about the heartfelt letter he'd written to her before he married Freda. When he'd agreed to Aden's offer, he had been determined that Leanna would hear the news from him instead of through friends and neighbors. Though he couldn't explain in the letter the real reason he'd made the decision to become Freda's husband, he'd asked Leanna to forgive him for any pain he might have brought her.

Might have?

The urge to laugh at his own foolishness choked him. Maybe he didn't deserve to be forgiven when he'd hardened his heart to the truth of how his choice—the one he'd believed he should make to repay the debt he owed to Aden for being a *daed* to him and Michael— had injured the woman he loved.

He wished he could reach out to God for comfort

and guidance, but how could he hope for help when he'd turned his back on his Lord like a petulant *kind* who hadn't gotten what he wanted?

I needed You then, Lord. Why did You ignore me? It was a prayer he had made often over the past year.

"Sometimes you're a mule-headed fool."

The voice that emerged from the darkness made him jump out of his seat. A second later, he recognized the voice as his brother's.

"Hello to you, too," he said to hide his reaction that he'd been getting an answer directly from God.

Michael set his hat on a peg by the door and crossed the room, being careful to skirt the twins.

His brother scowled. "*Ja*, sometimes you're a mule-headed fool, Gabriel, and the rest of the time you're just plain stubborn."

"So you've said. About a million times."

"Well, maybe the millionth-and-first time will be the time when you'll listen."

"I'm not going to argue with you when I don't have any idea what's got you so hot under the collar."

"I'm annoyed for the same reason you're sitting here pouting in the dark." He put his hands on the table and leaned forward. "Leanna Wagler."

"What about her?"

"Why are you doing everything you can to push her away? It's not like she's flirting with you or making your life miserable by reminding you how you tossed her aside so you could marry Freda." Michael shook his head. "Something—I've got to say—that, after having met Leanna, I can't understand why you did. Leanna is a special woman, and you were *dumm* not to marry her when you had the chance."

"It's not something I can explain."

"Yeah, yeah." Michael grimaced. "All that stuff about the heart leading the head or other sentimental garbage. I think it's an excuse for your desire for drama. If things get too quiet, you try to shake things up by shaking poor Leanna up. I can't believe you treat a woman you say you care about like that."

"I don't—"

Michael flung up his hands. "Don't tell me you don't know what you've done. Benjamin's sister, Sarah, was at their house tonight, and she was upset. She said Leanna had enough to deal with without you adding more stress to her life."

"Michael—"

"I don't want to hear it, Gabriel. You messed up the first time around with Leanna, but for some reason I can't fathom, she's stepped up to help with your *kinder*. You welcomed her into our home, so what was she to think but that you're interested in her again? What are you interested in, Gabriel? Having a make-believe family that's convenient for you?" He didn't give Gabriel a chance to answer. Putting his scowling face close to his brother's, he snarled, "What happens when it's not convenient any longer?"

"Michael, it's not what you think."

"Isn't it? Well, it doesn't look as if it'll be much longer, because you're messing everything up again. Do you know how few people get a second chance to right a wrong? And you're throwing this one away!"

His brother stormed out of the kitchen and up the stairs. As Gabriel returned to the table, he heard Michael's boots slamming on the floor upstairs.

Heidi gave a soft cry of alarm.

"It's okay," Gabriel said to soothe her and her brother. "Your *onkel* Michael likes to be loud sometimes." He made a silly face, which made the *bopplin* smile before they began playing again.

Folding his arms on the table, he pondered what his brother had said. Michael was right…from his point of view. Without knowing the whole truth, his brother saw him as a witless *dummkopf.*

And maybe he was.

Could his brother be right about him pushing Leanna away by resorting to drama?

A knock on the door startled Gabriel. Who was calling so late at night?

Whoever it was must be carrying a flashlight, for he saw it move when the person knocked a second time. He got up and opened the door.

"Leanna, what are you doing here?" he asked as he motioned for her to come in.

She took a single step into the kitchen and closed the door behind her. As she stepped into the light, he saw the raw emotion on her face that matched her broken voice when she said, "My *grossmammi* needs surgery on her heart."

Leanna's heart longed for Gabriel to take her into his arms and hold her until her fear faded away. When she'd gotten home from the hospital with her *grossmammi*, and while *Grossmammi* Inez got ready for bed, she'd spent time explaining to her siblings what they'd learned. Leanna had gone out to check on her goats, wanting time alone to unwind from the appointment, and instead, she found herself walking to Gabriel's house.

No matter how irritated she was with him, no matter how little she comprehended why he'd chosen Freda over her, there was a bond she'd never been able to explain between her and Gabriel. Something that went beyond friendship, beyond obligation and even beyond love. It was as if, in times of trouble, he was the one she must turn to.

Gut sense rallied in time, so she bent to pick up the *bopplin*. Without a word, Gabriel took Heidi from her and put his other hand on her arm. He opened the door and steered Leanna toward the rocking chair on the front porch. She didn't resist, so tired from trying to appear cheerful for her *grossmammi* that she wasn't sure how much longer her knees would hold her up.

Once she was sitting, rocking slowly, he pulled the other chair near to where she stared out across the yard toward the horizon and the faint silhouettes of the Green Mountains. She loved the view from his porch, and tonight she'd be happy to lose herself in watching the stars dance across the sky. She appreciated the reminder that she was small in the universe and that God was holding her beloved *grossmammi* in His hand.

"Inez needs surgery on her heart," he said, prompting her to speak.

Leanna cradled a sleepy Harley in her arms, the pace of her rocking increasing as she outlined what the *doktor* had said less than two hours before. "She must have a new valve to replace a clogged one. I asked about pills, but the *doktor* said it would only postpone the surgery and delaying could be stupid because the valve is getting more clogged. It's making *Grossmammi* Inez weaker and weaker. If she gets too weak, the surgery will become extra dangerous."

"So she has no choice."

"Not if she wants to feel better."

He sighed as he looked at Heidi, who was falling asleep against his chest. "Where are they going to do the surgery?"

"Albany."

"That's, what, forty miles from here?"

"More than fifty. We'll arrange for a driver, Hank if he's available, to take us there." She waved that aside as if that detail weren't important.

"What will the *doktors* do during the surgery?"

"It's almost unbelievable. They've made so many new medical advances, and what they can do is awe inspiring. They'll send the new, man-made valve through a vein in her leg, knock the old valve aside and set the new one in place."

"You're right. That sounds crazy, but I've heard about other types of procedures that use veins to reach the patient's heart. When are they doing the surgery?"

"Day after tomorrow. We've got to be there before seven, because the surgery is scheduled for around ten in the morning. Juanita will come over that day to take care of the *bopplin*. I hope they behave for her."

"Don't worry about it. I've—"

She didn't let him finish, too focused on what needed to be done to pay attention to what he was saying. "To be honest, Juanita is looking forward to it now that the twins know her better. Juanita told me to let you know that she'll be available for as long as necessary to babysit. My brother Lyndon's wife, Rhoda, as well as Sarah and Miriam, will take care of Juanita's housecleaning jobs until she can return. I don't know how long *Grossmammi* Inez will need me. Once she's home again, if you can drop off Heidi and Harley, I'll watch them at our house while I'm helping my *grossmammi*."

"I told you. You don't have to worry about the twins."

"Of course, I do. I told you that I'd babysit for you, and I don't go back on my word. If I did, then why would anyone believe what I said ever again? I…" Her eyes widened as if she'd realized that what she said could have been considered a slur aimed at him. "Gabriel, I didn't mean…that is…" With a groan, she put her hand over her face.

He took her hand and lowered it. "You don't have to apologize for speaking the truth, Leanna. I let you believe one thing, and then I did the opposite. I should be astonished that you have done as much as you have for me and my family after what I did."

"What you did was marry someone else. You didn't make any promises to me."

I wanted to make you a promise that would last a lifetime.

The words burst into Gabriel's head like an explosion. The memory of his brother's sharp words followed. Instead of helping Leanna as she was helping him, he was filling her life with more strain and uncertainty. When she should have been thinking of her *grossmammi*, she'd been making plans for childcare for him.

"Leanna, you don't need to worry about the twins," he repeated.

Her brow furrowed, creating deeper shadows in the dim light from the kitchen. "What do you mean?"

"I know you agreed to watch them as a favor, and I've taken advantage of your kindness for too long. That's why I've found someone else to watch them." He'd tried to explain that to his brother, too, but neither Michael nor Leanna had given him a chance.

"Someone else?" She stiffened in the chair, and Harley roused with a soft complaint.

"David Bowman's *mamm* has been looking for something to do now that his *kinder* are getting older, and I know you're overwhelmed with helping here along with everything else you do. She's volunteered to get the *milch* from your house and make the *bopplin*'s formula. You've mentioned several times how you worry about Inez doing that because the least little thing tires her out."

"Annie's been making the formula before she goes to work at the bakery most mornings."

"So it'll be easier on your twin, too."

And easier on me.

He bit back the words he shouldn't speak. He didn't want to admit that Michael was right, that he hadn't looked for a substitute before because he'd wanted Leanna to come to the house every day. That Gabriel liked having the woman he had almost married help him create his make-believe family.

In front of him, Leanna seemed to wilt. The strength she'd shown tonight and every day since they'd met again drained from her. What had happened? He'd thought she'd be pleased with his solution to easing her stress.

He opened his mouth, but she halted him by coming to her feet. She handed a half-asleep Harley to him and straightened her shoulders. No warmth brightened her face as she looked down at him.

"That sounds like a reasonable solution, Gabriel." Her voice was crisp and her words clipped. "Shall I finish out the week?"

"That's not necessary. With Inez's surgery coming up in a couple of days, it'd be better if Magdalena started right away. That way, if she's got any questions, I can have her talk to you before you get involved in caring for your *grossmammi*."

Turning on her heel, she bade him goodbye as she'd done at the end of every day she'd been at the house.

Unlike then, she wouldn't be returning.

He watched her vanish into the shadows.

"So are you pleased with yourself?" Michael asked through the open door.

Gabriel didn't answer. He should be relieved. Leanna hadn't made a scene or given him more than a token argument. She'd been gracious as she always was, keeping her feelings private.

No, that wasn't true. He'd seen the flash of hurt in her eyes before she'd hidden it.

Everything had gone better than he'd hoped.

So why did he feel as if he were the greatest and most heartless *dummkopf* who'd ever walked God's green earth?

Chapter Fifteen

The morning air was close and sticky when Leanna stepped out onto the back porch. She was relieved Juanita had agreed to milk the goats this morning. Annie would be teaching Magdalena Bowman how to make the formula for Harley and Heidi, but her twin was useless when it came to milking either the goats or the cows. Annie loved animals and was always sneaking treats to Penny whenever the copper-colored pup came into the house, but she hated milking. She was happiest when she was working at the bakery, devising new recipes with the man she'd be marrying in the fall.

In spite of herself, Leanna looked across the dark fields to where she could barely see the tilting silo behind the Millers' barn through the glistening gray of morning fog lit above by moonlight. She wondered if the brothers would fix it or tear it down and build something new.

Then she wondered why she cared.

Gabriel had been pushing her away for the past week, and she'd been too *dumm* to realize it. She'd sought him out because she thought he'd offer her some comfort in the wake of her *grossmammi*'s prognosis. Instead, he'd told her that he'd found someone to replace her in taking care of his *kinder*. She shouldn't be surprised after the debacle when he decided to marry Freda, but she'd been so sure there was more to him that the self-serving man she didn't want to believe he was.

She'd been wrong.

"Ready?" asked a weak voice from behind her.

Turning, Leanna offered *Grossmammi* Inez her arm. That the older woman took it as they went down the steps warned Leanna that her *grossmammi* was feeling worse. Glad her *grossmammi* wouldn't have to suffer through another day of gasping for breath, Leanna sent a quick prayer to ask God to guide the surgeon's hands and instruments with skill.

They'd reached the grass when a vehicle turned up the driveway and came to a stop near where the buggy was parked. In the light from the porch, the van was spotlessly white, and Leanna wondered how Hank managed to keep it so clean on unpaved roads. The short man with gray hair and a beard turning to the same shade jumped out of the driver's side and came around to open the passenger doors.

"Good morning, ladies," he said, cheerful as always. He wore his usual coat that, he'd told Leanna months ago, was purple and gold to support the local high school teams. Without asking, he assisted *Grossmammi* Inez into the van.

Leanna appreciated the *Englischer*'s kindness and how he didn't make a big deal of how her *grossmammi* sounded as she breathed or how she shuffled when she walked. After climbing in to sit beside *Grossmammi* Inez, she thanked Hank when he closed the sliding door before going around the van and getting behind the wheel.

Though she'd given him the address when she contacted him, Leanna told him again that they needed to go to Albany Medical Center.

"The New Scotland Avenue entrance?" he asked.

After he'd switched on the light in the van, she checked the map among the papers her *grossmammi* had been given by the surgeon's staff. *"Ja."*

"Let's go. It's already almost five thirty." He smiled at them as he turned off the light and turned the key in the ignition. "I'm glad we're leaving so early, so we shouldn't have to worry about too much rush hour traffic on our way."

Leanna leaned against the hard seat and watched her *grossmammi* wave to their family gathered by the driveway. She knew their cheerful expressions were as false as her own.

There wasn't much traffic on the road into Salem, but the small talk she made with Hank drifted away before they'd gone ten miles. Beside her, *Grossmammi* Inez was looking out the window at the houses and barns rushing past in the strengthening light of the day.

"I haven't ridden in cars often," the old woman said as they wound through the streets of Greenwich, which were draped in the fog that had grown thicker while they followed the road along the Battenkill. "It reminds me of the motion picture I saw when I was a young girl. Everything moved so fast. I scarcely had time to see one thing before something else had replaced it."

"I didn't know you'd ever gone to a movie."

Her *grossmammi* wagged a finger at her. "I know I seem as old as these hills to you, *kins-kind*, but there were movies fifty years ago." She winked at Leanna. "And I know exactly how many you and your sister managed to sneak out to see with your friends. Three."

"Ja." She tried to laugh, but it sounded fake even to her. "We never could fool you, *Grossmammi* Inez."

With a pat to Leanna's arm, she said, "Now, now, don't sound so sad. I'm not planning on leaving this life today. In fact, the *doktor* said replacing the valve should make me feel two decades younger. I plan to stick around here so I can spend a lot more time with my *kins-kinder* and your own *kinder.*"

"I know." She blinked tears away, but others rushed to take their place and threatened to fall down her cheeks. "I want you to know how much we appreciate what you've done for us."

"I love you, so the rest was easy."

"You opened your home to us when first *Daed*, then *Mamm* and Bert, our stepfather, died, and you raised us when you could have been enjoying your retirement."

Her *grossmammi* made a sound that sounded like something Heidi did when offered something to eat that she despised. "Retirement? Sitting on the porch and rocking and watching the sun rise and set? Such a boring life would have led me to an early grave. You *kinder* have kept me on my toes and kept me young."

"You could have—"

"No, Leanna, there's been nothing else I would have wanted to do. Having so much time with my *kins-kinder* has been a *wunderbaar* blessing that I wouldn't trade for anything." She patted Leanna's cheek. "And I re-fused to let you *kinder* be separated."

"Separated?"

Grossmammi Inez waved a diffident hand. "There was a lot of talk about where all of you would live after your parents died. You know how everyone feels the need at such times to voice an opinion. Nothing ever came of it. I shouldn't have said anything. After all these years, what does it matter? We are where God wants us to be, and that's together."

Leanna gave her *grossmammi* a gentle hug, not wanting to squeeze her and make it more difficult for her to breathe. If *Grossmammi* Inez wasn't so anxious about the surgery, she most likely never would have mentioned that there had been a discussion to place the Wagler *kinder* in different homes.

The rest of the long ride to Albany was mostly silent, though Leanna answered whenever her *grossmammi* spoke. She wasn't surprised when *Grossmammi* Inez grabbed her arm and didn't let go when the van zoomed across a high bridge. Her *grossmammi* kept holding on to her when they exited onto narrow city streets with cars that seemed to go as fast as on the highway.

"There's the hospital ahead of us," Hank said.

Leanna peered through the windshield at a tall redbrick building. Cars were jammed up in front of the entrance. She glanced at the clock on the dashboard. They would never reach the office in time to check in if they had to wait for those cars to clear.

"Don't worry." Hank glanced back with a smile. "We're going into a different parking lot. We'll have you there with plenty of time to spare, Inez."

"We can be dropped off at valet parking," Leanna reminded him.

"Even better."

The van zipped around the corner and then took a quick right. A sign, Valet Parking Here, was a welcome sight because it confirmed they were in the right place.

She didn't wait for Hank to open the door for her. She slid it aside and stepped out to go around the van and help her *grossmammi*. She heard a frantic siren and saw a crimson ambulance race to a door about a hundred yards away.

Salem Rescue Squad was painted in large white-and-gold letters on the side.

She stared as the passenger door opened and a familiar form jumped out. She had to be wrong, but how could she mistake Gabriel Miller for any other man?

Behind her, she heard Hank draw in a sharp breath.

"Go," urged her *grossmammi*, and Leanna guessed that reaching the hospital had made *Grossmammi* Inez's stress worse. "Check...while they...get me a...wheelchair to...take me...upstairs."

"I should—"

"Go! Don't...argue...with me." Though *Grossmammi* Inez's voice was breathless, her strength of will remained powerful.

Leanna kissed her *grossmammi*'s cheek and promised to join her upstairs. The old woman waved her away before taking Hank's outstretched hand so he could help her out.

Rushing across the grass between the two entrances, Leanna reached the emergency room door as a gurney with an impossibly small cargo emerged from the ambulance.

"Gabriel!" she shouted.

He whirled and stared at her in astonishment. "Leanna?" he asked as if he couldn't believe his own eyes.

"What are you doing here?" she cried.

"It's Harley." His face was long with despair. "You were right, Leanna. There's something wrong with him. Something horribly wrong."

Gabriel pushed aside the heavy door and walked into the surgical waiting area. A half-dozen people sat in the room decorated with cheerful prints and posters show-ing cutaways of the human heart. His gaze focused on one person.

"May I?" he asked, motioning to the empty chair next to where Leanna sat.

She nodded and swallowed roughly. Was she trying to hold in that mixture of fear and sorrow and recrimi-nations that threatened to gag him?

"How is Inez?" He settled himself in the uncomfort-able chair and noticed how nobody other than Leanna would meet his gaze. They, like he, must wish they could be, at that moment, anywhere else in the world but waiting to hear if their loved one had survived surgery.

"She went in half an hour ago. They said they'd come and get me in about an hour or so."

"They can finish her surgery so fast?"

"That's what they said." Dampening her lips, she whispered, "Why are you in the cardiac surgery wait-ing room?"

"They're doing an exploratory to find out what's wrong with Harley's heart."

Her fingers slid over his on the narrow arms of the chairs and curled around them. The motion said more than any words could have, and warmth trickled through him, like the first sign of a spring thaw after a frigid winter.

"I'm so sorry," she whispered. "What happened?"

He was amazed she hadn't asked the question before. Realizing he hadn't given her a chance before he rushed into the emergency room with Harley, he sighed. "He stopped breathing."

"Oh, my!" She became even more gray with fright.

"He and Heidi were sitting on the floor, and she crawled away. He started to follow, made it a foot or so, then collapsed. I shouted for Michael, and he went for help." He stared at his clasped hands. "I picked Harley up and patted his back like I've seen you do when he's gasping. He didn't respond, so I patted harder. He began breathing, but not well. His lips were blue, and his fingertips were turning blue by the time your friend Sarah burst into the house."

"Sarah is a volunteer EMT."

"I am so thankful she was at your house when Michael went there to find out the closest place with a phone. She got Harley breathing steadily again and kept working with him until the ambulance arrived. She told me to go with him, and she'd make sure Heidi was okay. I jumped in the ambulance and came here to the emergency room. He needs surgery, which they hope will keep him from stopping breathing like that." He bowed his head. "It was terrifying. He's such a tiny *boppli*."

Fear smothered him, and he couldn't hold back the tears that had been dammed within him since the day he'd known he must break Leanna's heart in order to protect the only family he had. When she put her arms around him, he gripped her arm. He wept against her shoulder, hoping his scalding tears didn't sear her. He no longer cared there were others watching.

She didn't pull away and, instead, leaned into him, putting her cheek against his hair. She said nothing, and he was grateful she didn't try to give him a list of platitudes. He knew them. He'd probably said each of them at one time or another.

Trust in the doktors. *They know what they're doing.*
Have faith and hope for the best.
God doesn't give us more than we can handle. That one contradicted what he'd been told after Aden's death.

God knows when it's our time because we are each a precious piece of His plan.

He believed those were true, but hearing them wouldn't help. The only things he wanted to hear were that Harley and Inez had come through their surgeries.

As the last of his tears fell, Leanna whispered, "I'm sorry, Gabriel."

"You can say that you told me so." He raised his head and girded himself for the sharp words he deserved, the words she should have thrown into his face weeks ago.

She took his right hand and folded it between her smaller ones. Meeting his gaze, she whispered, "What *gut* will that do?" Her eyes were almost turquoise with the tears welling up in them, and he knew they were for Harley and him. "Harsh words aren't useful at the best of times."

"Which this isn't."

"No, it isn't." She glanced at the double doors that stood between them and the surgical area. "They told me it wouldn't take that long for *Grossmammi* Inez's surgery, but it seems like I've sat here a lifetime already."

"Are you here alone?"

She nodded. "*Grossmammi* Inez insisted only one of us come. As I can hand off my chores and I'm not working out of the house, she asked me to come."

Gabriel fought to swallow again. There hadn't been any accusations in her words, but they both knew the truth. If he hadn't acted like a cowardly *dummkopf* and hired Magdalena to watch the *kinder*, Leanna would have been on her way to his house that morning and one of her siblings would have been sitting in the waiting room.

"Who's watching Heidi?" she asked, showing that her thoughts must be close to his. "Magdalena?"

"Sarah insisted on taking her to your house so she'd be nearby when I got home. Annie was there, or so Michael told me before we left." He gave her a faint smile. "I guess it takes two people to handle your job."

"More likely Sarah had planned to visit Annie today, and they'll watch Heidi together."

"Either way, I appreciate their stepping in to help, especially when your sister has to be anxious about Inez's surgery."

"And Harley's." Her face grew a bit paler. "They don't know about that, do they?"

"I've got the phone number at the bakery. I called and left a message about what the *doktors* have decided. I'll call when he's out of surgery. If you want, I can let them know about Inez, as well."

She patted her black purse. "Annie gave the phone number to me, along with instructions to call the minute I know how our *grossmammi* is doing."

"There's a phone we can use not far from the elevator."

"The cardiac unit has a phone for people who don't have cell phones. We can use it to share news with our families. One of the local church groups in Albany had it installed. I was told I could use it to call for a ride, too. If you're ready to leave when I am—"

"I appreciate that, but I can't make any plans until Harley is out of surgery."

"I know." She hesitated, then went on, "I wish I'd been wrong about Harley. However, if I'd had any idea it was so serious, I would have been insistent, even if it annoyed you."

"And I'm sorry, Leanna, I didn't listen to you. I know your concern comes from your love for the *bopplin.*"

"That's true. *Danki* for understanding."

"Eventually."

She gave him a crooked smile. "Better late than never...or so I've heard."

Leanna was paging sightlessly through a magazine when the doors to the recovery area opened yet again. Each time they had, she and Gabriel—along with everyone else in the waiting room—had sat up straighter, willing that the name the nurse called to come back would be theirs. The waiting room had emptied, and other people had come in, but the ninety minutes Leanna had been supposed to have to wait had been over almost forty-five minutes ago.

"Wagler?" called the nurse, a tall, dark-skinned man who wore light blue scrubs that were almost the same shade as her dress. His name identified him as Darnell.

She suddenly was unable to move or speak. All at once the wait time seemed to be too short, because she feared what the nurse might tell her. And how could she leave Gabriel here alone when his son was on the operating table?

"Over here," Gabriel said. Turning to her, he urged, "Go ahead. Inez will be wondering where you are, and you don't want her to worry. That won't be *gut* for her heart."

"But—"

When he took her hand between his much larger ones, he looked directly at her so she couldn't doubt his sincerity. "Go ahead, Leanna. I'll be fine."

"If you hear anything about Harley..."

"I'll send word to you right away." He squeezed her hand, then released it.

"Promise?"

"I keep my word."

"I know." And she did know, though she'd tried to ignore the fact before. For those he cared most about, Gabriel would keep his word, even if it made him look bad. His brother had said Gabriel always kept his promises, and she wondered what ones Michael was talking about. Whatever they were, they'd exacted a great toll on Gabriel's soul, a price he was still paying. That he'd never once complained told her that she had never met anyone else with such strength.

God, hold him up. He loves You, too, I know. His faith is wobbly, but I know it must be at least as big as a mustard seed, and Your son told us such small faith can move mountains.

Leanna kept praying for Gabriel, for her *grossmammi*, for Harley, for herself, for the others who were in the hospital. She followed the nurse into the recovery area. There was a mixture of urgency and yet calm in the wide space that had rooms with curtains across the opening that connected them to the central space. Men and women went from one room to the next, pushing equipment she couldn't identify. It was hushed, though she heard quiet voices in the rooms she passed.

Darnell stopped in front of a curtain covering the entrance to the fourth room on the right. Opening it, he said, "Mrs. Wagler, you've got a visitor eager to see you." He gave Leanna a compassionate smile. "Go on in."

"Is she—?"

"I'm all right," her *grossmammi* said faintly.

She looked past the gurney in the center of the space to a female nurse who nodded to confirm *Grossmammi* Inez's words, and then Leanna realized *Grossmammi*

Inez had spoken without all the pauses that had slowed her speech since almost the beginning of the year.

"She needs to rest here in recovery for a few hours. No getting up or moving around so she causes bleeding on her incisions." According to the tag on the female nurse's scrubs, her name was Judy. "After that, we'll move her upstairs and monitor her overnight. If everything is as it should be in the morning, you can take her home then."

"So soon?"

"Amazing, isn't it?" Judy closed the top of a laptop sitting on a shelf with items Leanna couldn't identify. She smiled as she picked up a cup and offered *Grossmammi* Inez a drink of water through the bent straw. "I see these surgeries every day, and I marvel at what our doctors can do."

After Judy left, Leanna pulled a chair to a spot where her *grossmammi* could see her without moving. She wasn't surprised *Grossmammi* Inez's first question was about Harley.

Leanna told her only that the *boppli* was being examined by the *doktors*. She didn't want to upset her *grossmammi* now, and she wasn't sure how much medication *Grossmammi* Inez was taking. The anesthesia hadn't completely worn off.

"Gabriel said he'll let us know how Harley is doing as soon as he knows."

"Ach," her *grossmammi* moaned. "Such a little *boppli*." Holding out her hand, she turned her head when Leanna took it. "We are two voices, but there must be many more in Harmony Creek Hollow raised in prayer right now. Let's join them."

Leanna bowed her head as she reached out with her heart. She heard the older woman's whispered words and repeated them. In addition, she thanked their Heavenly Father because her *grossmammi*'s voice seemed to grow stronger with each word she spoke. The pauses had almost vanished already. Leanna couldn't wait to call the bakery and share the *gut* news.

When *Grossmammi* Inez drifted to sleep, Leanna alerted Judy that she was going to call her family. She glanced into the waiting room when she walked past, but Gabriel wasn't there. Was Harley out of surgery?

She didn't hear anything from Gabriel before it was time to move her *grossmammi* to her room for the night. Judy reassured her. If Gabriel sent word about Harley's condition to the recovery unit, they would pass it along to *Grossmammi* Inez's room.

Not if, Leanna wanted to argue. *Gabriel promised to let me know as soon as he could. He never breaks promises.*

As the time passed while her *grossmammi* seemed to get better by the minute, Leanna sat in a chair by the bed and began to wonder if Gabriel had forgotten his promise. She couldn't believe that, but why else hadn't she heard anything? Was it possible Harley was still in surgery? She was going to have to return home soon because *Grossmammi* Inez must get what sleep she could. The older woman wouldn't rest while Leanna was there.

When an aide brought in a supper tray, Leanna knew she couldn't put off calling Hank any longer. She started to stand, but halted when a young man in bright green scrubs came in. His badge identified him as a nursing student.

"Miss Wagler?" He stared at her, and she guessed he hadn't ever seen a plain person before.

"I'm Leanna Wagler."

He thrust a folded piece of paper at her. "I was told to give this to you."

"*Danki*. Thank you."

Nodding, he rushed out, and she heard him asking someone at the desk why she was dressed so strangely.

"Aren't you going to open it?" *Grossmammi* Inez asked while she took the lid off a plate of meat loaf and mashed potatoes.

"*Ja.*" Her fingers trembled as she unfolded the page. It was a simple message that gave her a room number that was in a different section of the hospital and a scrawled note: *Please come. Gabriel.*

"What is the news from Gabriel?" asked *Grossmammi* Inez.

"He doesn't say. He sent me a room number. It must be where they brought Harley after his surgery."

"What are you waiting for? Go ahead," her *grossmammi* said as Gabriel had earlier. "Don't leave for home without letting me know how the *boppli* and his *daed* are doing."

"I won't." She gave her *grossmammi* a kiss, then rushed out of the room. She was already praying by the time she reached the elevator.

Chapter Sixteen

The hallway was brightly lit, and people moved with unhurried determination to complete tasks Leanna couldn't begin to comprehend. Outside the row of doors, computers displayed information that seemed to be updating constantly. The walls were decorated with pictures of animals and carnival rides and cartoon characters she'd seen at the grocery store.

The faint protest from a *kind*, quickly hushed, wafted toward her, but most of the rooms she passed were silent. She guessed the *kinder* were asleep by now. Odors of disinfectant and other cleaning supplies assaulted her senses, and she fought to keep from sneezing as she walked along the hall.

Checking the numbers on the doors, she slowed as she neared the one that matched the number Gabriel had sent her. She was shocked that everybody in the unit couldn't hear her hammering heartbeat. She took a deep breath to steady herself.

She tiptoed into the room. It was dim compared to the hall, and she paused to allow her eyes to adjust so she didn't bump into something or someone. Out of the shadows, the silhouettes of furniture appeared. A chair.

A table on wheels. A crib. The soft beeping from a machine matched her anxious heartbeat. In astonishment, she realized the steady sound must be Harley's heartbeat.

As she started to thank God, she heard Gabriel speak. He stood by the crib, his hands on the rail as he gazed down at a tiny form on the mattress.

"Have pretty dreams, sweet Harley," he said. "Sleep easy tonight and for the rest of your life. I'll be here for you each one of those days that God grants me. I promise you, no matter what happens, I'll be your *daed* forever."

"Of course you will," Leanna said before she could halt herself. "Why wouldn't you always be his *daed*?"

Gabriel straightened and faced her. "How is Inez?"

"As tart as a barrel of dill pickles." She smiled as she shared the amazing news. "She's stronger and acting more like herself than she has in a year. With the new heart valve, it's almost as if she's a brand-new woman. I'd say she'll give a woman half her age a run for the money by the end of the month."

"That's *wunderbaar*."

Though she wanted to ask why he hadn't answered her question, Leanna looked at the crib where Harley was motionless. "How's he doing?" she whispered.

"Sleeping, which the nurses tell me is the best thing for him. The procedure went even better than they'd hoped, and they told me there's *gut* reason to believe it'll be the only one he'll ever need. Like your *grossmammi*, he'll have to see a cardiologist at least a couple of times a year." He gave her a half smile. "Maybe we can arrange for them to go together."

"She would love that. You know how she adores *bopplin*."

"As you do."

"*Ja*. I…" She clasped her hands behind her before she could reach out to take his. While she walked over to the window that gave a view of the building across the street, she knew he was watching her. He was waiting for her to continue, but she wasn't sure what to say.

Footsteps, hushed but assertive, came into the room, and Leanna saw a trim dark-haired woman dressed in scrubs with the some of the same cartoon characters as on the walls in the hallway.

"Hi! I'm Sally." She glanced toward the crib. "I'm the RN for that handsome young man over there." She was careful not to use Harley's name so she didn't rouse him from his healing sleep. "I'll be here for you and for your son tonight, Mr. Miller. If you've got any questions—any questions at all—don't hesitate to ask. Or ask Alan. He's the LPN here tonight."

"*Dan*—thank you," Gabriel said as he stepped aside to let Sally examine the sleeping *boppli*.

When she was finished, she said, "He's doing well. You've got a beautiful son." She checked the computer she held before adding, "And he'll be more beautiful and strong now that his heart isn't fighting against him."

"What happens now?" Leanna asked.

Sally glanced at Gabriel, who nodded that it was all right to answer Leanna's question. "Children with his condition live long and normal lives. There may be a few things you'll want to check with his doctor about before he does them, but moderate exercise and play shouldn't be a problem for him. The important thing is to keep in touch with your son's cardiologist through the years, so the problem doesn't become serious again."

Leanna moved closer to Gabriel and put a hand on his shoulder. He glanced at her before looking at Sally and asking when his son would be able to return home.

"You can discuss that with his doctors when they make rounds in the morning. With little ones, we have to be more patient, because they can't tell us if they're feeling better. We need time to observe how he's doing before we can make that decision." She gave them a warm, professional smile. "Don't hesitate to call if you've got any questions."

Gabriel thanked the nurse. He'd lost count of how many people he'd thanked since he'd been taken to the pediatric recovery unit. The staff had been kind and explained everything to him about the surgery, which hadn't been so different from Inez's, though more delicate because Harley was such a young *kind*. There had been talk of putting him in the pediatric ICU overnight, but his vital signs had rallied and he'd been brought to this room, which contained the monitors and other devices he needed.

As soon as he'd had a chance, Gabriel had written a note to send to Leanna. He'd been reluctant to take her away from her *grossmammi*, but knowing how worried she'd become if he waited any longer, he'd arranged with one of the staff to have it delivered to Inez's room. That had been almost three hours ago, so he guessed the note had gone a roundabout route to reach her.

Now she was here, and he couldn't imagine anyone else he'd want beside him.

"Leanna," he said at the same time she murmured, "Gabriel."

"Go ahead," she urged.

"Let's sit over by the window so we don't disturb him." Like the nurses, he didn't use the *boppli*'s name. "It'll be better to talk there. The nurse said he'll sleep through the night, even when she comes in to check him, but I don't want to risk waking him."

He let her take the rocking chair while he got a folding chair from the hall and set it beside her. Though he wanted to hold her hand as he had in the waiting room, he didn't reach for it.

"I've had a lot of time to think about a lot of things," he said. "Mostly I've been thinking about how you deserve to know the truth."

"What truth?"

"All of it." He leaned toward her. "I know you realized after Michael's remarks at your sister's graduation that Freda was pregnant when we got married." He looked toward the crib, then at her. "What I'm about to tell you nobody else alive knows. Not even Michael. I made Freda and her *daed* a promise that I wouldn't ever speak of why I married her."

"You told me she was pregnant, so I guess you married her to protect her family name."

He gave her a sad smile. "That's true, but there's more to the story than anyone, other than me, knows. I want you to know, too."

"You said you promised not to speak of it, and you always keep your promises."

"I do, and I promised to keep this one so it wouldn't hurt the Girod family, but after I prayed on it—"

"You prayed to find the answer? You reached out to God?" Her face lit with pure happiness. "Oh, Gabriel, I'm so happy you've found your way back to God."

"I am, too. I'm thrilled all I had to do was open my heart to Him, and He was there."

"He always was."

"I know." Awe warmed his voice. "Or I should say, I know that now. It's such a blessing God has patience with His most stubborn *kinder*."

"With all of us, whether we're stubborn or not." She set her hand on his arm. "Gabriel, I'm happy for you."

Placing his hand atop hers, he was amazed how right it seemed to be sitting with her. "It was through talking to God that I realized telling you the truth won't break the promise I made. Nothing I say to you will wound either Aden or Freda, because they are safe from pain with our Heavenly Father."

"I'm listening," she said as she took a deep breath. She was, he knew, preparing herself for whatever he had to say.

He sandwiched her hands between his. "What I did was for love, but not the love of a man for a woman. I never saw Freda that way. She was always like a little sister to Michael and me. Aden made us feel a true part of their family from the day he opened his door to us. Not once did he do or say anything to make us feel that he loved us any differently than he did Freda."

"That's how it's been with *Grossmammi* Inez. She believes she's been blessed to raise another family when she could have stepped aside." She swallowed hard. "She refused to let us be sent to different family members because she wanted us raised together."

"I think that's why Aden took us in, too. Though I was very young, I seem to remember people talking about which family should take Michael and which should take me. I was terrified because I couldn't imagine growing up without my brother." He glanced toward the crib. "I pray Heidi and her twin never have to know such fear."

She drew one hand from between his and cupped his cheek. "Don't falter in your belief that he's going to be fine. The *doktors* have fixed him up as *gut* as new. Better. That's what the nurse said."

He took a jagged breath, knowing his faith needed

time to grow as strong as hers. For so long he'd been hiding from people, not trusting even God, never knowing who might convince him to break his promise to Aden. With God freeing him and Leanna believing in him, he was sure he'd found the right way to go.

"When Aden came to me and asked his favor, I knew I had to agree," he said, watching her face.

"A favor? I thought he would have been upset because you and Freda had…" She colored prettily.

"We didn't, Leanna."

"But she was pregnant!" She clapped her hands over her mouth as her voice rose.

"*Ja*, she was, but I'm not the *bopplin's daed*."

"What? They live with you."

"I'm raising them, but I'm not their…what's the word? I'm not their biological *daed*."

"But they've got your red hair."

"Which is why no one's questioned that they're my *kinder*. I never knew Aden Girod's wife, but I'm guessing she was a redhead, too."

"I don't understand. Why did you marry Freda, then?"

"Because the *Englischer* who is the twins' actual *daed* refused to marry her. Once we were married, the *kinder* would be seen by the community as belonging to me. Aden thought that would protect his daughter and his *kins-kinder*. He knew he didn't have much more time to live, because his lung cancer had spread throughout his body." He held his breath as he waited for her answer.

He needed her to understand why he'd made the decision he had. If she didn't, he wasn't sure he could stay in Harmony Creek Hollow and be near her day after day and never have a chance to hold her. In the past few days as she'd treated him like an employer and nothing more, the idea of watching her marry another man had become a burning poison in his gut.

"Oh." She clasped her hands in her lap. "That makes sense."

He laughed with relief. Of all the answers he'd anticipated she'd give him, that hadn't been one of them. It sounded like Leanna, sensible and caring and empathetic.

"I hope I'm as *gut* a *daed* to these *bopplin* as Aden was for me and Michael. We might not have shared a blood relation, but he was a true *daed* to us."

"As you are for Heidi and that sweet *boppli* over there."

"I wish I could have told you the truth in the letter I sent you."

Her eyes widened. "The letter?"

"I explained as much as I could within the constraints of the promise I'd made. I'd hoped you would read between the lines and know that I hadn't made the choice without realizing how much it would hurt you. Did it help you?"

Leanna cleared her throat, but had to fight to get her words to emerge as she whispered, "I never read your letter."

"What?" His eyes grew wide as his brows shot upward. "Didn't you get it?"

"I did, but I didn't read it. I threw it away unopened."

He stood and shook his head. "You threw it away unopened? I spent hours on it. I wrote and rewrote and crossed out and started over from the beginning while I tried to find the right words to ask for your forgiveness, though I couldn't tell you the whole truth." He jammed his hands into his pockets. "All this time, I've been thinking that I must have written something so terrible there was no chance you'd ever forgive me."

She gazed at him, her voice breaking. "I couldn't read it, Gabriel. To read you didn't love me as I loved you would have been like rubbing a file across sunburned skin."

"I didn't write that."

"What did you write?"

"It started out this way. 'My dearest Leanna,'" he murmured as he leaned forward and ran his fingers against her soft cheek. "I wrote at least a dozen pages, though I sent you only two. Nothing I wrote could say what I wanted to."

"And that was?"

"How sorry I was I never had the chance to ask you to marry me."

She gasped. "You were going to ask me to marry you?"

"Ja." A shy smile eased the lines of worry from his face. "I'd hoped that once I'd bought you a big dish of ice cream—"

"I planned on having a hot-fudge sundae."

"And I was planning to ask you as you finished the last bite if you'd sweeten my life by becoming my wife."

She bit her bottom lip to keep it from trembling. "I'd hoped you might, but then you married Freda, and that changed everything."

"You're right. Nothing is the same as it was the day we were supposed to meet for ice cream."

"We have moved far from Lancaster County, and you've been blessed with two *bopplin.*"

"And you've become more beautiful and your heart warmer." He walked away to look into the crib. "I know I can't ask you to be my wife."

"Because you don't love me?"

Shock emblazoned his face. "I've loved you since the night you first let me drive you home. I've never stopped loving you, and I never will. You're a *wunderbaar* woman. You deserve a man who'll be a *gut* husband for you. That's not me."

Getting up, because she was too shocked to sit, she asked, "Why would you say something like that?"

"I failed Freda by not being there when she needed me."

"You did what you could. You spoke with her *doktor*, and you listened to advice. You offered her your name and a life together."

"I couldn't offer her enough."

She crossed the room and put her hand on his arm. Stroking those strong muscles, she whispered, "You're right."

"I am?" His face lengthened again.

"*Ja.* Nothing you could have done was enough because her heart was broken, and you weren't the one who could repair it. Trust me on this, Gabriel. I know far too much about broken hearts."

Again he walked away from her, but this time she didn't follow. She watched as he paced. He must be trying to sort out what were new ideas for him. When he stopped, he stood right in front of her.

"I'm going to have to get used to you being right all the time, Leanna."

"I'm not right all the time. Nobody is."

"You're right about this. Freda had a picture of an *Englisch* man lying beside her when she died. I think it was the twins' *daed*."

"You can compare it to Harley when he's grown.

Maybe you'll see something in the photo to confirm your guess."

"I can't."

"You got rid of it?" She could understand why he would have thrown away the picture of the man who'd hurt Freda so much.

He shook his head. "No, I slipped it into Freda's coffin just before the top was closed. I knew she would have wanted the man she loved with her forever as he was at her last breath."

Tears fell from her eyes. How could he think he wasn't a *gut* man? How could he believe he hadn't been the best husband he could have been to Freda, who had longed for another man? Gabriel's final loving act for the woman he'd described as his beloved little sister was to give her in death what she couldn't have in life.

Leaning her head against his arm, she whispered, "*Ich liebe dich*, Gabriel Miller. I have from the moment I first saw you and I won't ever stop."

"You're a fool to love a man like me."

"*Ja*, I'm a fool if loving a man who has opened his heart to two adorable *bopplin* and their *mamm* is foolish. I'm a fool if loving a man who honored the *daed* who raised him by granting him one of his last wishes is foolish. I'm a fool if loving a man who loves me is foolish."

"I do love you. I've never stopped loving you." He gathered her into his arms.

His lips found hers as easily as if he'd kissed her as many times as she'd dreamed he had, warm and gentle and persuasive and filled with longing. Their second kiss, which had been so long delayed, put her dreams to shame, and she melted against him. Her breath caught as he deepened the kiss. She had waited so long for this kiss, and she knew every moment of the uncertainty and sorrow had been washed away by the love swelling through her.

"Will you marry me, Leanna Wagler?" he asked. "Will you be my wife and the *mamm* of my *kinder*?"

"You know that's the first time I've heard you call the twins 'my *kinder*.'"

"Are you avoiding giving me an answer?"

She smiled as she locked her hands behind his nape. "Now you know how it feels!"

"Leanna!"

"Of course, I'll marry you. How could you doubt that for a second?"

"Because I'm always surprised by you."

A soft sound came from the crib, and they turned as one to look at Harley, who was shifting in his sleep.

Though she wanted to stay with the man she'd never believed would be hers, she said, "I should go and see how my *grossmammi* is. The *doktor* wants her to rest tonight, and she won't if she starts wondering why I've been gone so long. I don't want her heart to get beating too fast."

"Then you'd better not tell her about this." He drew her into his arms and kissed her again.

She locked her fingers behind his neck as she gazed up at his beloved face. "I'm going to tell her and the whole world about this. No more secrets for you and me, Gabriel. We've had too many for too long."

He grinned broadly. "I agree, and, to be completely honest, I don't think I can keep how much I love you a secret from anyone anyhow."

Her laugh faded as he drew her closer again. As he kissed her, she knew he was right. Something as amazing as their love could never be a secret.

Epilogue

Leaves crunched beneath Leanna's sneakers and the wheels of the red wagon as Gabriel pulled it along the twisting road that led to the far end of Harmony Creek Hollow. Inside the wagon, the twins chortled as they tossed leaves at each other. Harley had grown faster than his sister in the past three months, and they were almost the same size. He'd surprised everyone by walking before Heidi had.

"He's trying to make up for lost time," was what *Grossmammi* Inez said. Like the little boy, she'd recovered from her surgery and seemed to live every minute to its utmost. She no longer had to gasp for breath after each word, and she had reclaimed the kitchen as her own, delighting in making meals for her family. Once again, she sat with the family in the evening and read from the Bible, so they could pray together before bed.

Leanna took a leaf away from Heidi before the little girl put it in her mouth. Heidi tried to put everything in her mouth while Harley was more intent in trying to figure out how their toys could be taken apart. He'd been tearing leaves into tiny pieces, and their clothes and hair were littered in red and gold that glittered in the last light of the day. The sun set earlier with each passing day as summer faded into fall.

Today would always be one Leanna remembered with a warm glow because today was the day she and Gabriel had spoken their vows as husband and wife in front of the community. In the morning, the four of them would be leaving to visit relatives in Lancaster County.

"I think the *kinder* will enjoy riding on the train to Pennsylvania," Gabriel said as he reached down to brush some leaf bits out of his son's hair.

"Entertaining them for eight hours will be a challenge."

"Bring plenty of cookies and books for them to color in." He chuckled. He did that more and more, and she savored each laugh. "Assuming they don't try to eat the crayons again."

"Last time they drew on each other's faces and hands."

"As they did with icing from the wedding cake?" He laced his fingers through hers as they walked together. "It was a *wunderbaar* wedding dinner."

"Between Annie's cooking and Caleb's baking skills, there couldn't be any complaints."

"Your friends seemed to find a lot of the day funny."

She hesitated, then realized she needed to be as forthcoming with him as he'd been with her the day of the two heart surgeries. "They were celebrating because the members of our older girls' club aren't eligible for it any longer."

"Why?"

"Because we called it the Harmony Creek Spinsters Club."

"Spinsters Club?" He laughed and slid his arm

around her waist. "You're going to have to pass that title on to other women."

"No, it's better to retire the name. Let others come up with a name for their groups of friends."

"Or we could have the Harmony Creek Bachelors Club now that Michael is spending so much time with Benjamin and Menno Kuhns."

"I don't think they'd appreciate being called that."

"Which makes it all the more fun to use." He chuckled, a sound she knew she'd never tire of hearing.

"I'm glad you told Michael about Freda."

He grew serious. "I am, too. What amazes me is that he wasn't surprised. He said he knew there had to be some overpowering reason why I didn't marry you in the first place."

"Our siblings know more than we give them credit for." She paused in the road. "Here we are."

"At Eli and Miriam's house? Why are we here?"

"You'll see." She took the handle of the wagon from him. *"Komm mol."*

Leanna led the way to the barn beyond the house. She smiled and waved to Miriam, who stood beside Eli's nephew, Kyle. The boy, who'd sprouted up several inches over the summer, was grinning.

"Are you ready to see them?" Kyle asked.

Enjoying Gabriel's puzzled expression, she followed Kyle into the barn and to a corner where a blanket peeked over the edge of a large wooden box. She looked in and asked, "Which one?"

"This one." The boy lifted out a black-and-white puppy and handed it to Leanna.

She carried it to Gabriel. "I know she'll never be the dog that you had to give up when you were a boy, but I thought she'd make a *gut* wedding gift for you."

"She's the perfect gift," he said, his voice breaking. "I only told you that story once, but you remembered."

Touched by his reaction, she hurried to say, "She's too young yet to leave her *mamm*, but by the time we return from visiting family and friends, she'll be ready to join our family. Harley and Heidi are going to love her."

Gabriel took the puppy from her and knelt by the wagon. The adoration between the twins and the little puppy was instantaneous, and Leanna didn't know which one wiggled more in excitement as the *bopplin* reached out to pet the puppy's silken fur. Both twins began to giggle with excitement, and the puppy's tail wagged so hard it was a blur.

Blinking abrupt tears, Leanna sent up a prayer of thanks that Harley could laugh and not lose his breath. In the four months since his surgery, strength had flowed through the little boy as his heart pumped life along his veins.

The *bopplin* and the puppy protested when Gabriel stood.

"How about you, Leanna?" He handed the pup to Kyle. As the boy set her in the box, Gabriel said, "You're the one who'll have to train her and clean up her puddles until she's housebroken."

"Puddles! That's a cute name."

"I hope you'll think so after a couple of weeks of having three *bopplin*—two human and one puppy—in the house along with having to take care of your goats."

"I know I'm going to love everything about our home together."

Not caring that Miriam and Kyle were standing on the other side of the wagon, because, after all, it was her wedding day, Leanna gave her husband a swift kiss.

She started to step away, but his arm around her kept her close.

"If you'll excuse us a minute, Miriam," he said with a wink, "my wife and I have some lost time we need to make up for."

"You may need more than a minute." Miriam laughed and motioned to her nephew to come with her. They walked out of the barn.

"She's right," he said as he bent toward Leanna again. "We're going to need a lifetime."

"Starting now?"

He answered her with a sweet kiss, and she knew she would love every moment of the rest of their lives together. Some things, she'd learned, were worth the wait.

* * * * *

If you enjoyed this story,
don't miss the other books in the
Amish Spinster Club series
from Jo Ann Brown:

The Amish Suitor
The Amish Christmas Cowboy
The Amish Bachelor's Baby

And be sure to pick up these other exciting
books by Jo Ann Brown:

Amish Homecoming
An Amish Match
His Amish Sweetheart
An Amish Reunion
A Ready-Made Amish Family
An Amish Proposal
An Amish Arrangement

Find more great reads at
www.LoveInspired.com.

Dear Reader,

Life's twists keep us on our toes, don't they? Leanna and Gabriel never expected they'd meet again. However, they came to realize you can't escape your past by fleeing it and that they needed to trust God was leading them back to each other.

In our lives, we may try to be like Leanna and Gabriel. We try to keep our pasts in our past and hold on to secret and not-so-secret hurts. It's only when we face those fears that we can truly move forward.

Thank you for sharing the stories of the Amish Spinster Club. These books have been a special treat for me because they're in my hometown. I hope you've had fun visiting Salem and Harmony Creek, too.

Visit me at www.joannbrownbooks.com. Look for my new Amish series, set in beautiful Vermont, coming soon.

Wishing you many blessings,
Jo Ann Brown

COMING NEXT MONTH FROM
Love Inspired®

Available July 16, 2019

THE AMISH BACHELOR'S CHOICE
by Jocelyn McClay

When her late father's business is sold, Ruth Fisher plans on leaving her Amish community to continue her education. But as she helps transition the business into Malachi Schrock's hands, will her growing connection with the handsome new owner convince her to stay?

THE NANNY'S SECRET BABY
Redemption Ranch • by Lee Tobin McClain

In need of a nanny for his adopted little boy, Jack DeMoise temporarily hires his deceased wife's sister. But Jack doesn't know Arianna Shrader isn't just his son's aunt—she's his biological mother. Can she find a way to reveal her secret...and become a permanent part of this little family?

ROCKY MOUNTAIN MEMORIES
Rocky Mountain Haven • by Lois Richer

After an earthquake kills her husband and leaves her with amnesia, Gemma Andrews returns to her foster family's retreat to recuperate. But with her life shaken, she didn't plan on bonding with the retreat's handyman, Jake Elliott...or with her late husband's secret orphaned stepdaughter.

A RANCHER TO REMEMBER
Montana Twins • by Patricia Johns

If Olivia Martin can convince her old friend Sawyer West to reconcile with his former in-laws and allow them into his twins' lives, they will pay for her mother's hospital bills. There's just one problem: an accident wiped everything—including Olivia—from Sawyer's memory. Can she help him remember?

THE COWBOY'S TWIN SURPRISE
Triple Creek Cowboys • by Stephanie Dees

After a whirlwind Vegas romance, barrel racer Lacey Jenkins ends up secretly married and pregnant—with twins. Now can her rodeo cowboy husband, Devin Cole, ever win her heart for real?

A SOLDIER'S PRAYER
Maple Springs • by Jenna Mindel

When she's diagnosed with cancer, Monica Zelinsky heads to her uncle's cabin for a weekend alone to process—and discovers her brother's friend Cash Miller already there with his two young nephews. Stranded together by a storm, will Monica and Cash finally allow their childhood crushes to grow into something more? _____

LOOK FOR THESE AND OTHER LOVE INSPIRED BOOKS WHEREVER BOOKS ARE SOLD, INCLUDING MOST BOOKSTORES, SUPERMARKETS, DISCOUNT STORES AND DRUGSTORES.

LICNM0719

Get 4 FREE REWARDS!

We'll send you 2 FREE Books plus 2 FREE Mystery Gifts.

Love Inspired® books feature contemporary inspirational romances with Christian characters facing the challenges of life and love.

FREE Value Over **$20**

YES! Please send me 2 FREE Love Inspired® Romance novels and my 2 FREE mystery gifts (gifts are worth about $10 retail). After receiving them, if I don't wish to receive any more books, I can return the shipping statement marked "cancel." If I don't cancel, I will receive 6 brand-new novels every month and be billed just $5.24 for the regular-print edition or $5.74 each for the larger-print edition in the U.S., or $5.74 each for the regular-print edition or $6.24 for the larger-print edition in Canada. That's a savings of at least 13% off the cover price. It's quite a bargain! Shipping and handling is just 50¢ per book in the U.S. and 75¢ per book in Canada.* I understand that accepting the 2 free books and gifts places me under no obligation to buy anything. I can always return a shipment and cancel at any time. The free books and gifts are mine to keep no matter what I decide.

Choose one: ☐ **Love Inspired® Romance Regular-Print** (105/305 IDN GMY4)   ☐ **Love Inspired® Romance Larger-Print** (122/322 IDN GMY4)

Name (please print)

Address   Apt. #

City   State/Province   Zip/Postal Code

Mail to the Reader Service:
IN U.S.A.: P.O. Box 1341, Buffalo, NY 14240-8531
IN CANADA: P.O. Box 603, Fort Erie, Ontario L2A 5X3

Want to try 2 free books from another series! Call 1-800-873-8635 or visit www.ReaderService.com.

SPECIAL EXCERPT FROM

Love Inspired®

What happens when the nanny harbors a secret that could change everything?

Read on for a sneak preview of
The Nanny's Secret Baby,
the next book in Lee Tobin McClain's
Redemption Ranch miniseries.

Any day she could see Sammy was a good day. But she was pretty sure Jack was about to turn down her nanny offer. And then she'd have to tell Penny she couldn't take the apartment, and leave.

The thought of being away from her son after spending precious time with him made her chest ache, and she blinked away unexpected tears as she approached Jack and Sammy.

Sammy didn't look up at her. He was holding up one finger near his own face, moving it back and forth.

Jack caught his hand. "Say hi, Sammy! Here's Aunt Arianna."

Sammy tugged his hand away and continued to move his finger in front of his face.

"Sammy, come on."

Sammy turned slightly away from his father and refocused on his fingers.

"It's okay," Arianna said, because she could see the beginnings of a meltdown. "He doesn't need to greet me. What's up?"

"Look," he said, "I've been thinking about what you said." He rubbed a hand over the back of his neck, clearly uncomfortable.

Sammy's hand moved faster, and he started humming a wordless tune. It was almost as if he could sense the tension between Arianna and Jack.

"It's okay, Jack," she said. "I get it. My being your nanny was a foolish idea." Foolish, but oh so appealing. She ached to pick

Sammy up and hold him, to know that she could spend more time with him, help him learn, get him support for his special needs.

But it wasn't her right.

"Actually," he said, "that's what I wanted to talk about. It does seem sort of foolish, but…I think I'd like to offer you the job."

She stared at him, her eyes filling. "Oh, Jack," she said, her voice coming out in a whisper. Had he really just said she could have the job?

Behind her, the rumble and snap of tables being folded and chairs being stacked, the cheerful conversation of parishioners and community people, faded to an indistinguishable murmur.

She was going to be able to be with her son. Every day. She reached out and stroked Sammy's soft hair, and even though he ignored her touch, her heart nearly melted with the joy of being close to him.

Jack's brow wrinkled. "On a trial basis," he said. "Just for the rest of the summer, say."

Of course. She pulled her hand away from Sammy and drew in a deep breath. She needed to calm down and take things one step at a time. Yes, leaving him at the end of the summer would break her heart ten times more. But even a few weeks with her son was more time than she deserved.

With God all things are possible. The pastor had said it, and she'd just witnessed its truth. She was being given a job, the care of her son and a place to live.

It was a blessing, a huge one. But it came at a cost: she was going to need to conceal the truth from Jack on a daily basis. And given the way her heart was jumping around in her chest, she wondered if she was going to be able to survive this much of God's blessing.

Don't miss
The Nanny's Secret Baby *by Lee Tobin McClain,*
available August 2019 wherever
Love Inspired® *books and ebooks are sold.*

www.LoveInspired.com

Looking for inspiration in tales
of hope, faith and heartfelt romance?

Check out **Love Inspired**® and
Love Inspired® Suspense books!

New books available every month!

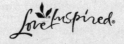